Dragon Blood Chronicles 1: Oath

Dragon Blood Chronicles 1: Oath

Avril Sabine

Cracked Acorn Productions
Australia

Dragon Blood Chronicles 1: Oath

Published by

Cracked Acorn Productions

PO Box 1365

Gympie, Queensland 4570

Australia

978-1-925617-07-8 (Kindle)

978-1-925617-08-5 (Print)

Genre: Young Adult Urban Fantasy

Cover design by Caitlyn Petersen

For my kids, who said, "You need just one more Dragon Blood story. Well, maybe a few more."

Sometimes you fight hardest against what you need most.

When Claire and her father move to a new house, she refuses to believe the rumours about Roy, the boy next door. It doesn't take her long to realise she should have listened. She's thrown into a world where only the strong survive, discovering a secret Roy has spent his life fighting against. She's determined to not only survive, but find her place in the dangerous world of dragons, Mages and Knights.

*

This story was written by an Australian author using Australian spelling.

Name Pronunciation

Like many names there is more than one way to pronounce the following ones. These are the pronunciations used in this story.

Names:

Liana (lee-ah-nuh)

Rian (ree-in)

Ronan (row-nen)

Other pronunciations:

Pliethin (plea-thin)

Temolae (tem-oh-lay)

Chapter One

Claire glared at the small, white dog that looked more like the head of a mop than an actual living creature. "Give me a minute and quit making so much noise." She fumbled with the lock, wishing she could have had that last fifteen minutes of sleep.

The door finally swung open and the dog ran into the backyard, his high pitched yips continuing. Claire slipped her feet into the sneakers beside the door and stumbled after the dog, muttering under her breath as she drew her jacket closer around her pyjamas. "So unfair. Mum gets a honeymoon in Europe and what do I get? Being stuck with you for a month." She shivered in the cool morning air, hardly able to believe it'd be spring in ten days. It didn't seem possible it was almost September. "Bub! What are you doing?" She tried to keep her voice low. There were sure to be people asleep at this hour. Who wanted to get up before six on a Saturday morning? Certainly not her. The sun hadn't risen yet. She glanced skywards. Although it couldn't be far off with how much the sky had lightened.

Claire lunged for the dog. "Got you." She swore when the dog escaped, heading straight for the broken palings leading to the house next door. "Bub!" When the dog continued to ignore her, she finally gave in. "Bubbles." She glared when he turned towards her, tail wagging and mouth hanging open. "Stupid name." She scooped up the dog. "Why can't you answer to something more dignified? Mum should be banned from naming anyone or anything." Look at the name she'd given her.

Movement caught her attention and she peered through the broken palings that were half hidden by overgrown shrubs. Her gaze was drawn to the young man pacing in the neighbouring backyard. She hadn't met him, only caught a few glimpses of him during the week they'd been here. She guessed he was around her age of seventeen, possibly a little older. He was dark skinned with broad shoulders and a shaved head.

Why was he pacing in his backyard? Several times he looked towards the sky, barely pausing in his pacing. A smile slowly formed. Maybe it wouldn't be so bad living here, even with the extra twenty minutes it'd take to reach school each day. She automatically reached up to try and neaten her sleep mussed, sun streaked, long brown hair, nearly dropping the dog. Bubbles wriggled and Claire tightened her grip, turning away after one more glance at her neighbour.

Reaching the back door, she struggled to get it open while trying not to let Bubbles escape. She didn't set the dog down until they were in the laundry and the external door was closed. Leaving her jacket on, she slipped off her sneakers and wandered into the kitchen, knowing she'd have to face the cold again shortly when she saw her dad off to work.

Darrell placed his breakfast dishes in the sink, turning to her with a worried look in his dark eyes, already wearing his hi-vis work shirt. He tried to run a hand through his black hair that was too short, these days, for him to be able to do that. "Are you sure you'll be all right?"

She almost tripped over Bubbles. Giving the dog a glare, she crossed the room and hugged her dad. "Quit worrying. I'll be fine. You didn't go on this bad the first time I stayed home alone." Back when she'd got sick of Bentley's lectures and Jacqueline trying to turn her into someone she wasn't. Other than looks, except her eyes that were the same dark brown as her dad's, she wasn't in the least like her mum and not interested in being like her. Nor did she think being told 'you're such a tomboy' was an insult. Even with the exasperated tone her mum used. "I've been doing this for more than a year, Dad."

"It's different this time." He held her at arm's length, his hands on her shoulders. "You're not as grown up as you think. What if something goes wrong? Your mother won't be here if you need help."

She grinned. "It's probably that I'm more grown up than you wish."

"You're not about to start on that dating thing again, are you? That boy is too old for you. He's in uni."

"Dad." She drew the word out. It wasn't that she'd really wanted to date the guy. It had been more about being told she couldn't, even before she'd considered it. "Are you really going to give me a lecture before you head off for two weeks?"

Darrell sighed, drawing her close for another hug. Letting go, he stepped back, a half smile forming. "All right. But you make sure you ring and leave a message for me at the mine office if anything happens. Anything at all."

She rolled her eyes. "Yes, Dad." The words were

spoken with exaggerated patience. As if she could forget with the amount of times he'd told her. "Anyone would think this was the first time I'd stayed at home on my own."`

"It's not like it's a small country town where everyone knows everyone else. Brisbane is a city." He grabbed his medium sized cloth suitcase, the seams frayed from years of use.

She walked beside her dad as they headed for the front door. "Really? I would have sworn it was a small country town after listening to Harold from over the road. That old man must have nothing better to do than spy on the neighbours and make up stories about them." Stepping outside, she drew her jacket close, the sun now rising. Her feet instantly chilled when she stepped onto the concrete path. She should have put her sneakers on again, but they'd been at the back door.

"He told me yesterday that the neighbours on that side," he pointed to the right, "are in a gang."

She snorted. "Yeah right. Like the old lady at the end of the street is a drug dealer?"

Darrell chuckled. "Just because he was wrong about Jean doesn't mean he's wrong about this lot." He nodded towards the neighbour's place. "He said there was a shoot out there at the start of the year."

She thought of the dark skinned boy she'd seen in the backyard. "I bet he only says that because of their skin colour. Like he probably said Jean is a drug dealer because she's Asian. Harold's got more prejudices than anyone else in the world."

"I wouldn't go that far. But how about you wait until I'm home before we meet the rest of the neighbours." His gaze was drawn to the four-wheel-drive that pulled up. "You take care and behave." He wrapped one arm around her, the other hand holding his bag. "And no more fighting at school."

She drew away from him. "Have you heard any complaints?"

He tugged on the sleeve of her jacket to reveal part of a bruise on the side of her forearm. "Are you going to tell me that you've become accident prone?"

"That's a defensive mark. Not an attack one." She tugged her sleeve back into place.

"Who threw the first punch?"

"You're holding Rick and Tina up." She waved to her dad's mate and his wife, who was driving the vehicle. She smiled when they waved back, glad she didn't have to make the drive out to the airport to drop her dad off.

Darrell sighed. "Stay out of trouble."

She grinned at him. "When do I get into trouble?"

He glanced over his shoulder to the vehicle. "We don't have time for the full list." He took a couple of steps towards the road. "Ring me if you need me."

"I'll be fine. Go." She watched him head towards the vehicle, smiling when he paused to stare at her before he got in the back seat. She could almost hear him telling her to behave. She waved in answer and waited until the vehicle was out of sight before she returned inside, her feet feeling like blocks of ice.

Silence filled the place and she started to head towards her bedroom, determined to get those fifteen minutes of sleep she'd missed out on. Hearing Bubbles' high pitched barking, she felt like growling. Would that dog ever shut up? So much for getting a bit more sleep. She strode towards the back door, glaring at the dog as soon as she stepped into the laundry.

"What's your problem now?"

Bubbles continued to jump and scratch at the door, barking and whining.

"You've not long been out there." When the dog continued, she sighed heavily. "Fine. But next time Mum thinks she can ditch you with me I'll be telling her no. You can stay at the kennels." Her threat was empty. Hopefully Bubbles didn't realise. Slipping her feet into her sneakers again, she opened the door and watched as Bubbles dashed outside, still barking. Closing the door behind her she wandered outside to keep an eye on the dog.

When Bubbles dashed for the broken palings, Claire ran after him. She managed to grab hold of his wriggling body before he could escape into the neighbour's yard. Her dad better fix the fence when he returned for his week off. She peered into the yard and saw the young man was still there, no longer pacing. Why was he standing around? It had to have been half an hour since she was last out here. Why would someone stand in their backyard doing nothing? It wasn't like he could be waiting for a bus.

A man appeared in front of him. He was tall, dark skinned, his dark brown hair was closely cropped, he wore leather clothes and had a sword at his side. Her jaw dropped and she nearly let Bubbles escape. Her grip tightened on the dog when he tried to wriggle away. Where had the man come from? He'd magically appeared and she wasn't some little kid who believed in magic. There had to be some trick involved. She strained to hear their conversation.

The man clapped the boy on the shoulder. "Think about it, Roy. We could do with people we can trust. There's been a lot of things happening."

"What sort of things?"

The man shook his head. "Nothing major, just little things. But there's been too many of them. Isaac thinks it's Knights trying to make up their minds after all the changes earlier this year. I reckon it's more than that. Someone wants his position. I think Silas wants to be the New South Wales High Protector."

"What does Lydia think?"

"That it's Claudia. Well, she said it'd more likely be Claudia than Silas."

"Did she actually agree with you about someone trying to take over?"

The man shrugged.

Roy chuckled. "Did she accuse you of being rash, Uncle Amos?"

"Never you mind," Amos muttered. He glanced towards the house. "Don't tell your mother I was here. Eliza would kill me if she knew I was asking you to come to Sydney."

"Does that mean I can tell Dad?"

Claire couldn't resist smiling at the humour she heard in Roy's voice. It faded as she once more tried to figure out what was going on.

Amos shook his head. "No, but your father doesn't scare me anywhere near as much as my sister." He reached out and clapped a hand on Roy's shoulder. He eyed him up and down. "Are you sick?"

"Recovering from dragon bone. You know what it's like. I can't avoid it all the time without making people ask questions."

Amos gave a single nod. "Take care. Let me know what you decide." He took a step away and vanished.

This time Claire did let Bubbles go, her mouth opening as she stared at the point where Amos had been. It wasn't possible. People didn't vanish. At least not like that. Her gaze was drawn to Roy who'd returned to his pacing, stopping as Bubbles raced towards him. He crouched beside the dog, scratching his stomach when he rolled over onto his back. Claire stared at Bubbles. She had to go over there and bring him home. Her mum would be pretty upset if she let anything happen to her dog.

It took her several minutes before she could bring herself to squeeze past the shrubs and broken palings and into the neighbouring yard. She froze when Roy looked in her direction. She met his dark brown eyes, a similar shade to her own, wishing she wore something other than her pyjamas and a jacket.

He rose to his feet, smiling. "I guess this one is yours." He gestured towards the dog that continued to lie on his back, wriggling in anticipation.

She nodded, remaining by the fence, trying to figure out how to ask him what trick his uncle had used to disappear. Every question she came up with sounded insane in her mind and would probably only sound worse spoken aloud.

Roy scooped up Bubbles. "I suppose you're one of the new neighbours." He strode towards her. "I'm Roy." He held out the dog.

She grabbed hold of Bubbles, clutching him tightly. "Claire." She had no idea what to do. Should she run? Slowly back away? Ask him what was going on? Roy seemed a lot larger close up. He had to be at least six foot. For the first time since she'd been staying home alone she wished her dad didn't work away for so long at a time. Either that or she was better at returning his missed calls and answering his emails.

"Do you need a hand fixing the fence?" He nodded towards the broken palings.

Shaking her head, she took a step backwards. No one would miss her. Not for days. Why hadn't she got in the habit of ringing her dad every day? Or several times a day.

"You don't say much, do you?" Roy's smile faded.

Normally she was more outspoken, but there was something about seeing a man disappear that was unsettling. She opened her mouth to speak. Three men appeared around them. Two had small timber cages, about seven centimetres square, hanging on chains with glowing orbs inside them. One of them had his hanging from his belt, the other man had hung a cage around his neck. They all went for Roy, who reached for his hip as if he expected a sword to be hanging there.

She stumbled back, prevented from going further by the paling fence. Bubbles escaped her grip and tried to attack the men. His high pitched barking rang out in the otherwise quiet morning and for once she wasn't tempted to tell the dog to shut up. If they were lucky, one of the neighbours might hear. The men tried to grab Roy, who fought with moves she'd only ever seen in movies. Nor had she seen them in her self-defence classes she'd taken on and off for a few years. She stood pressed against the fence, not knowing what to do. Maybe Harold was right and Roy's family were in a gang. Why else would he know how to fight like that?

One of the men turned away from Roy to look in her direction and she finally figured out what she should be doing. She ran. She didn't get far before a body crashed into her and she sprawled across the ground, cutting her hand on a rock edged garden bed. The sting was nothing compared to how bruised the rest of her body felt. She struggled to escape the man holding her down, Bubbles now attacking him. It was impossible to escape. Fear raced through her, causing her to struggle harder. The man shoved a cloth over her nose and a sharp smell filled her senses. She heard a man and woman shouting a moment before the world went black.

Chapter Two

Claire was woken by the sound of men arguing. It didn't take long for everything to come flooding back, especially with the aches and pains she felt throughout her body. She remained still, keeping her eyes closed. She had no idea where she was and didn't know if she should risk opening her eyes. Beneath her the floor was cold, hard and slightly damp. Her sneakers were missing and her feet were icy cold. Other than the sounds of the two men arguing, she heard nothing. She opened her eyes a crack and saw she faced bars. Fear raced through her and it was all she could do not to jump to her feet and demand they let her go. She saw two of the men from earlier. One was the man without a glowing orb and the other was the man who had hung his on his belt. He was now sitting at a small table with a single chair, not far from the bars.

The man who'd been without the orb pointed a finger at the other man. He was dressed in a black t-shirt and jeans, his dark brown hair cut close to his head and his brown eyes filled with anger. "I'm sick of being left behind, Wayne." He spun and strode towards a door on the far side of the room.

"What did you expect me to do? Think about it, Stanley. We couldn't leave the girl behind. She'd tell someone." He was larger than Stanley, the sleeves of his t-shirt tight around muscular arms. He had sandy brown hair that, like Stanley's, was little more than stubble.

Stanley turned to give Wayne one more glare before he strode from the room, not bothering to say anything.

Wayne stared after Stanley for a moment before he shrugged and stretched out his legs, leaning back in his chair. He'd barely got comfortable when his phone rang. He drew it from a pocket. "Yeah?" There was a pause while he listened to the other person. "I have no idea who she is, but we can use her as leverage to keep Roy in line. He's always been soft like that. A useless Knight. Not worthy of the name."

Claire wished she could hear what the other person was saying. She also wished she could look around and see what else was in the area. But she didn't dare move. When Wayne glanced in her direction she closed her eyes completely.

"No. They're still out to it. Okay I'll be up there in a minute to sort him out."

Hearing footsteps, Claire peeked through her eyelashes and watched as Wayne left by the same door Stanley had used. The glowing, caged orb remained on the table. When the door closed, she scrambled to her feet, wincing when her body protested against the aches and pains, the worst being her hand that bled slightly. A glance at Roy showed he remained unconscious, looking in worse shape than her with numerous cuts and gashes. She had to stay calm. It was the only way out of this situation. Isn't that what the different instructors had told her during some of her self-defence classes? Remaining calm was the only way to survive. That and being aware of your surroundings.

She scanned the room. The floor was concrete, what looked like mouse or rat droppings amongst the thin layer of dust. The walls were unpainted concrete block, the door across from the caged section was timber. There were no windows and the only light was a bare bulb in the ceiling above the table. She had no idea where they were or how they'd escape.

Checking the barred door, she found it was locked.

Another scan of the room showed nothing that could help. Her gaze was drawn to the timber cage on the table, the glowing orb caught inside. She had no idea what the orb was, but it didn't look like anything normal. It'd probably be up there with things like men vanishing in front of her.

Pressing herself against the bars, she reached for the cage. Her fingers grazed the edge. She stretched further, pushing hard against the bars, her breath drawing in sharply from the pains in her body. Her fingers hooked around one of the bars of the cage and she carefully tugged it towards the edge of the table where she was able to get a better grip on it.

It wouldn't fit through the bars. She sat on the floor to examine the caged orb, the cold of the concrete seeping through her pyjamas. There was a humming feeling coming from it and she held her breath as she pushed a finger between the timber bars of the cage. A prickling sensation caused her to draw her finger back. She examined her finger. It looked the same as always. Dirty, a few scrapes to go with the gash on her palm, but nothing was different. Letting her breath out in a long slow sigh, she closed her eyes a second before she pushed all her fingers into the orb. Nothing happened. Other than the prickling sensation. She opened her eyes.

What was it? And why was it in a cage? Like they were. She glanced at Roy. He remained still. Her gaze was drawn to the door across the room. Wayne and Stanley could return at any moment. And this little cage was obviously important to them. A smile slowly formed. They'd probably be upset if something was to happen to it. If she made sure she was too much of a problem, maybe they'd let her go.

Raising the cage, she slammed it against the concrete floor. The cage made a cracking sound, but held. She lifted it again.

"No!" Roy flung himself at her.

The cage connected with the concrete, breaking, the orb trying to escape. Her uninjured hand wrapped around it, a jolt of energy running through her at the same time as Roy grabbed her injured hand. She tried to pull from his grip when a burning sensation shot through her arm, radiating from her hand, more than the expected pain from a gash.

Her gaze connected with Roy's, seeing fear, pain and shock in their depths. Her mouth opened, but no words formed. The orb remained in her hand, the broken cage hanging around her hand and wrist. Roy continued to hold onto her other hand.

"Let it go." His words were soft, pain threaded through them.

She drew her hand through the bars, the cage coming with her, the orb feeling like it struggled to escape. "What is going on?" Her words came out softer than she'd planned. She'd wanted to demand answers from him.

"Let the Pliethin go." He continued to hold her hand, tightening his grip. "You have to-" He broke off, breathing in sharply.

"Roy?" Again she tried to tug her hand from his. This time it was so she could check the blood dripping down the side of his face from his temple, streaks of blood smeared across the rest of him from various cuts and gashes.

His eyes opened and he wrenched the Pliethin from her, continuing to hold her hand. He opened his mouth to speak, but all that came out was a jagged sound. He struggled to his feet, his grip on her hand momentarily tightening before it loosened.

This time when she tried to drag her hand from his, she was able to break free. "Roy." She rose, grabbing hold of him when it looked like he might collapse. Another jolt went through her and she nearly screamed, only the fear of catching the attention of Wayne and Stanley keeping the sound from escaping. She couldn't prevent a whimper. Letting go of Roy, she staggered back, stumbling and falling, landing hard on the concrete floor. Pain jarred through her and she looked up at Roy who seemed to be fighting against something, both of his hands clutching the Pliethin. She opened her mouth to speak, words failing her.

With another jagged cry, Roy transformed into a dragon, the change taking only a few seconds. His ebony scales were bathed in the gold light from the Pliethin, his claws grasping hold of the orb, his head thrown back, eyes closed.

She didn't know what to do, could only remain on the floor as she stared speechlessly at him. Dragons didn't exist. Just like men couldn't disappear. What was going on? Her head spun with crazy ideas and all she could do was stare up at the dragon who continued to hold the Pliethin. She would have expected dragons to be bigger, not the size of an extremely large horse or a small elephant. Not that she'd ever expected anything about dragons considering they didn't exist.

She had no idea how long she remained on the cold floor, Roy towering over her, before his eyes opened. The glow faded around him as he dropped to the floor, becoming human again, his clothes in tatters around him showing well-defined muscles.

He stared at the Pliethin that no longer glowed,

having become grey and misshapen. His hands opened and the Pliethin rose. "I'm sorry. I never planned to do this." The Pliethin faded until it vanished. He turned his gaze to Claire. "You should never have touched it."

She scrambled away from him, shrinking from his words. There'd been no threat in his voice, but that didn't stop her from wanting to escape. He'd been tall enough before, but it seemed that now he began to tower over her, becoming larger by the second. She had to get away, had to escape. She stumbled over soft ridges, scampering towards the wall. A frantic glance around showed no escape, the world unnaturally large.

"Change back. Before they return." There was an urgency to Roy's voice.

She had no idea what he was talking about. She looked down at her hands, squeaking when she saw they weren't human. Trying to move, she tumbled over, unable to walk without using her hands. Or what she now had instead of hands. She tried to scamper around, but Roy was quicker, scooping her off the floor, cradling her gently in warm hands. She peeked out of the cocoon he'd made, staring up at him.

"We have to escape. There's no hiding what I am.

Not with my clothes in tatters. If I let you go, will you help or run?"

She didn't know what she'd do and when she tried to tell him that, it came out as a squeak. This had to be a dream. Or a nightmare. There was no other explanation. The day had been filled with one impossibility after another. None of this could be real.

His thumb brushed across her back. "I'm sorry, Claire. You shouldn't be caught up in all of this. My uncles will help. If we can get out of here, and let them know what's going on, they'll help."

Another squeak was all she managed when she tried to demand what was going on.

Roy stared silently at her a moment. "None of this is your fault. No matter what happens I give you my oath that I'll protect you with my life. My oath as a Knight. Even if it takes letting others know what I am." He held her gaze. "But it'd be a lot easier to protect you if we could get away from here. I'd offer to turn into a dragon again, but it's not something I've practiced and I'm weak from the dragon bone I had recently." He paused a moment. "Can you understand me?"

Even though she didn't really, she nodded. She understood that they needed to get away from here and that she couldn't rely on him to protect her for all that he said he could. Well that was fine by her. She'd been looking after herself for more than a year and preferred it that way. Actually, she'd pretty much always looked after herself. Nate, her best friend, wasn't always there to watch her back and when he was, he more often led her into trouble than out of it.

"I'm going to set you down. Can you try and get under the door and see what is on the other side?"

She nodded, guessing he must have taken it for a yes when he placed her on the floor. A glance around had her wanting to run back to the cocoon of Roy's hands. Everything was so big. There was a pile of fabric to her left and she stared at it for a moment until she realised it was her clothes. She was naked! Squealing, she ran towards the door, figuring out halfway there that she was clothed in fur. But what about when she changed back? If she could change back. She hadn't even known she'd changed forms. How could she not have realised? You'd think something that monumental wouldn't go unnoticed.

Reaching the door, she squeezed under it, peering up and down a hallway. There were several closed doors and a set of stairs to her left. Scampering further into the hallway, her nose twitched at all the smells that reached her. Dampness, stale air, food, dust and other creatures. There were other smells, ones she couldn't place. When she tried to focus on any of them, they became a confusing mix. She ventured further away from the door, feeling vulnerable with how small she was. It was an uncomfortable feeling. One she was unaccustomed to. A glance back at the door had her taking a second look. A key was in the lock, another handful hanging from the key ring. Surely it couldn't be that simple.

She took a few steps back to the door, looking all the way up to the key. All right, it obviously wasn't going to be simple. Somehow she had to reach the key and use it to unlock the door. Her gaze was drawn to her hands, paws, then along her skinny, furred arms. There was no way she'd be able to do it as a mouse. She was going to have to figure out how to become human. A naked human.

Chapter Three

Claire took a deep breath. Ending up naked should be the last thing she was worried about. The bigger concern should be the men who'd grabbed them and planned to use her to keep Roy in line. How had she changed form? She thought over it. Shrinking away from Roy. She took another deep breath, feeling her whiskers quiver. The sensation distracted her for a moment before she forced herself to focus. Staring up at the keys, she reached for them, stretching out her little arm that was nowhere near long enough. She remembered reaching for the caged Pliethin earlier, stretching her arms through the bars, the pain of her bruises and the gash in her hand. She could feel them, but they didn't seem as bad as they'd been earlier, like they'd begun to heal. She stretched a little harder and the door handle came towards her in a rush, then it was below her.

Claire shivered, the hallway cold, the concrete floor adding to the coldness. She drew her hair around herself, but it did very little to warm or hide her nakedness. With one arm wrapped around her, she used her other hand to turn the key in the lock, opening the door slightly. Goosebumps rose on her body as the air around her shifted. She peered into the room. Roy held onto the bars, staring at the door she hid behind. "Push my clothes over to the bars and turn your back."

He did as she ordered, without hesitation, standing near the bars. "What is out there?"

She ran into the room, grabbed her clothes and pulled them on. Unlike Roy's clothes they were intact. She tugged her jacket around her, wishing she wore something better than her pyjamas under it. "You can turn around now."

"What is out there?" Roy nodded towards the open door.

"A hallway." She returned to the door and removed the bunch of keys, trying each of them in the door that prevented Roy from escaping. It was the second last one that worked. She should have started from the other end. Swinging the door open, she remained in the way. "What is going on?" Maybe she should have left him imprisoned until he'd answered her many questions. The ones who had captured him weren't necessarily the bad guys.

Roy took hold of her hand, looking down at it when she gasped. Cradling her hand, he stared at the gash that had stopped bleeding. "I'm sorry you were caught up in this." He met her gaze. "You have no reason to trust me, but I'm asking you to anyway. A Knight's oath is unbreakable."

"They didn't seem to think you were much of a Knight."

Roy grinned. "From them, I'll take that as a compliment."

Her gaze was drawn to his mouth. The smile he'd given her earlier was nothing compared to the way he grinned at her now. There was a touch of humour in his eyes. "Aren't you scared?"

His grin faded. "No." The word seemed to hang in the air for a moment. "They will not get away with this."

She drew her hand from his. "How can dragons exist?"

Roy took a step towards her, grabbing both her hands, holding the injured one carefully. "No one can know what I am." His voice was whisper soft, his head lowered towards hers.

"Why not?" She kept her voice equally low, meeting his dark brown eyes.

He didn't answer her immediately. "It'd put too many people at risk. Unless your life is in danger, and I have no other choice, I won't risk them." He met her gaze a moment longer before he glanced towards the exit. "We have to leave. We don't know how much time we have. Stay behind me and if you have the chance, run. Don't wait for me."

"Where do I run to?"

"Anywhere. Go home if you can, but I don't know where we are. We could be in a completely different country. Caged Pliethins allow them to quickly cross large distances."

She stared after him when he strode towards the doorway, a glance over his shoulder as if to ask what was holding her up. They could be in a different country? She ran after him. "What do you mean a different-"

"Quiet." He looked in both directions, breathing in deeply. "There are people upstairs. None down here." He began to open doors, checking in rooms.

She stepped in front of him when he walked out of one of the other rooms, identical to the one they'd been kept in. "How do you know?"

"Can we have this conversation later?" He moved

her out of the way, a glance over his shoulder to let her know to follow.

She hurried after him, staying in the next doorway. It was a bedroom, if such a sparse room could be considered to be one. There was a single bed, a chest of drawers and a built-in wardrobe. "Talk about budget interior decorating," she muttered.

Roy glanced at her, a grin forming as he took three daggers off the chest of drawers before striding to the wardrobe. He drew out a pair of black jeans and a charcoal coloured button up shirt.

Realising he was going to change into them, Claire turned her back. "You heard that comment?"

"I could have heard it if you had whispered it. Your hearing should be improved. And sense of smell."

Startled by how close his voice was, she spun to see he was behind her, dressed in the jeans and pulling on the unbuttoned shirt. She slowly shook her head. He was wrong. If anything her hearing was worse. Her ears felt blocked like she was at the top of a mountain and they wouldn't pop. And her sense of smell came and went, like she was coming down with a cold or something.

Leaving the shirt unbuttoned, Roy held out the bundle of his clothes. "Take these. And this." He held out a dagger once she'd taken the clothes.

"You'd have been better off giving me a stick." Taking the dagger, she smiled at the flicker of surprise that crossed his face. "Self-defence classes. One of the instructors said that sometimes the handle of a broom or a fallen branch might be all we had to fight off an attacker and taught us some moves." She stepped out of the way.

"Why aren't you screaming or falling apart? Not that I'm complaining."

"Because none of this can be real." She didn't know what it was, but that was one thing she was certain of. Dragons didn't exist and men didn't vanish before your eyes. Nor did people turn into mice. As real as all this felt, it had to be a dream or something.

"It isn't a dream."

For a moment she thought she might have spoken aloud. She followed him as he checked the last few rooms. "Then what is it?"

One of the rooms was locked and he had to use a key to open it. There was nothing different between it and the other bedrooms. It was equally as impersonal. Roy opened the built-in wardrobe to reveal numerous weapons.

Claire, who'd followed him into the room, gasped. She reached out to touch one of the larger rifles.

Roy stopped her before she could make contact.

"You don't want your prints on any of them. Who knows what crimes they've been used to commit." He closed the doors.

"We can use them to get out of here. You said there were people upstairs." She had no idea how to use a gun, but if it was a dream, that wouldn't matter. She was always more capable in dreams than she was in real life.

"No." Taking hold of her hand, he tugged her towards the last door along the hallway. It hid a cleaning supplies cupboard. Trying not to breathe, she stepped away, the smells overpowering. Typical that her sense of smell would momentarily come back now. "Who needs a dozen bottles of bleach?"

"Torturers."

She frowned, certain she'd misheard him. "What did you say?"

"It's good for cleaning blood off the floor." He closed the cupboard, striding towards the door at the top of the stairs.

Following him, she started to ask him if he was serious.

Reaching the top, he pressed a finger to his lips before he tested the handle. The door remained closed. He tried one of the keys in it, the lock clicking as he turned it.

Standing this close to Roy she felt the heat of his body and smelt the scent of his skin. She frowned. Her dreams never contained smell. Or taste. Fear rushed through her. It wasn't a dream. She had to remain calm. It was important to remain calm. And know the surroundings. Her breathing increased. She was stuck in a hallway with someone who had the ability to turn into a dragon, was wearing her pyjamas and holding a dagger, a bundle of clothes under her arm.

Roy turned towards her, his hands grasping her shoulders. "Breathe slowly. Don't fall apart yet."

She stared into his dark brown eyes, seeing the compassion in them. "Why is this happening? I want to go home." And she wanted her dad, but she couldn't say those words aloud without risking tears falling. "Bub could be anywhere. That stupid dog has no road sense."

"Take a deep breath. We are going to get out of here. There are three of them. I'll distract them while you run. Do you understand? Run."

She slowly shook her head. He wanted her to leave on her own? She'd never run from a fight in her life. And what was outside waiting for her? "What about you?"

"I'll be behind you as soon as I can. I'm faster than you. A lot faster."

The sound of raised voices caught her attention and she heard a handful of sentences. "Who is Amber? And why would she exchange herself for you?" He had a girlfriend? She tried to ignore the ridiculous feeling of disappointment that washed over her. All she should be worried about was getting out of here alive.

"Time to go. While they're distracted. Now remember. Run."

She didn't have the chance to tell him she wasn't good at running. She tended to stand and fight even when the sensible option was to go. It was why her dad had enrolled her in self-defence classes. Not so she could learn to fight, but so she could learn self-preservation and that running was an option. It hadn't helped.

Roy burst into a large kitchen, holding both daggers. Three men turned to face him, rising from the table they'd been seated around.

Claire remained frozen in the doorway, her gaze drawn to the guns the three men drew. She recognised two of the men. Wayne and Stanley. The third she remembered from when she was kidnapped, but didn't have a name for him. His sandy coloured hair was as short as that of the other two and his shoulders equally as broad. His green eyes narrowed as he looked at Roy.

"Why are you wearing my clothes?" Wayne demanded.

"He must be a dragon. There's no other way he could have escaped," Stanley said.

Claire saw Roy tense, remembering his words. No one could know what he was. It'd endanger other people. She stepped around him before she could think. "I ripped them up. I needed something to get us out of there." She grinned, the annoying bravado that tended to get her into trouble far too often, kicking in. "There was also the added bonus of seeing him naked."

Stanley's gun turned towards Claire. "Impossible. There was no way of getting out of that place with torn up clothes."

Her grin remained in place. "That's what you think."

Stanley's eyes narrowed. "You're a Dragon Mage?"

Roy took a step towards the men. "You aren't going to kill me. Amber won't trade herself for a corpse and she'll want proof I'm alive before she'll be willing to offer herself in exchange for me."

Wayne lowered his gun to point it at Roy's leg.

"Come any closer and walking will be an impossibility. A bullet through the kneecap won't kill you."

"Unless we don't bandage it." Stanley grinned as if he relished the idea of letting Roy bleed out.

Claire looked at each of the men. Were they for real? They'd shoot Roy in the kneecap? It was like a bad movie. Or at least Stanley was.

Roy stepped to the side before rushing at the third man. "Run!"

Chapter Four

Claire obeyed Roy's order, reaching the door and reefing it open. An ordinary backyard was in front of her, a large gum tree at the back fence, a cool breeze brushing across her face. It was late afternoon. Where had the day gone? Or was it even the same day? She took a single step forward, a gunshot causing her to look over her shoulder. Roy was pinned to the floor, a gun pressed against his head, Stanley grinning at him. Something in her snapped. She dropped the dagger and bundle of clothes, a roar escaping her throat as she rushed forward, her body seeming to change, the men growing smaller.

Stanley spun to face her, pointing the gun up at her. "Dragon." The word sounded like a curse.

She knocked the gun from his hand, spinning to attack Wayne when he drew a sword and came at her. Dragon? What was Stanley going on about? Roy had remained human. She picked up a chair, using it to block the blade coming at her. The fight was a confusing mix of sounds, smells and movement. The men seemed to be everywhere, their noise unbearably loud.

"Run." Roy staggered to his feet, pressing a hand to his side, blood seeping through the charcoal coloured shirt, a dagger clutched in his other hand.

Claire roared at the sight. They'd shot him? She barrelled into Wayne who stumbled over a chair that was lying on its side. The other man came at her and she swiped at him, shocked to see blood bloom across his shirt.

"No!" Roy launched himself at Stanley who'd picked up his gun and aimed it at Claire. He wrestled the weapon from Stanley, slicing him with the dagger.

Wayne wrapped an arm around the other man, who'd fallen, his fingers reaching for one of the two caged Pliethins sitting on the kitchen bench.

Stanley escaped from Roy, running towards Wayne. "You're not leaving me behind."

"Tobiah will bleed out if he doesn't get medical attention. Use the other Pliethin. Focus and you'll get the destination right this time." Wayne vanished from the room.

Stanley spun to face them, drawing the sword that hung at his side.

Claire remained frozen, her gaze on the claws that were coated in blood. Her claws. What was going on? A dragon? Hadn't she been a mouse before? Was she now an entire zoo? Including one of mythical creatures. A glance down and to her side showed deep, dark red scales that matched her wings, the veins a rose gold colour.

Roy gestured, with the gun, towards the caged Pliethin that remained on the kitchen bench. "You heard Wayne. Use it and get out of here."

Stanley hesitated.

"Unless you want me to shoot you in the kneecap so you don't follow us."

Claire turned her head to stare at Roy. Had he really said that? In such a conversational tone. He couldn't have been serious. She tried to speak, but only a roar came out.

Stanley bolted towards the caged Pliethin, grabbing it from the bench and plunging his fingers into the cage. He vanished.

Roy lowered the gun. "I was really hoping he wasn't a Knight Mage. Who would have been stupid enough to turn Stanley into one?" He faced Claire.

"You need to change back. We have to get out of here before they bring reinforcements."

She shook her head, unable to do as he suggested. She had no idea how she'd become a dragon. Or a mouse. Or even how to become a human again. Reaching for a doorknob wasn't going to work this time. None of them were out of reach.

Roy took a step towards her. "Remember what it's like to be human. Or at least that's what Am–" He broke off, starting again. "I've been told that's the easiest way to change back."

What it was like to be human? That was meant to be easy? It sounded like some sort of philosophical question. Did he want the answer to the meaning of life along with it? She growled in frustration.

Roy tucked the gun into the waistband of his jeans and reached for her, pressing a hand against her foreleg. "Close your eyes. Shut out all sounds and smells. Think about what it feels like to be in your skin."

She closed her eyes. The scent of blood grew stronger and she had the strange urge to lap it up. Revulsion rolled through her and she felt herself change, cold air caressing naked skin. Opening her eyes, she saw Roy shrug out of his shirt and wrap it around her.

He averted his gaze. "I'll see if there's any transport. We can't wander the streets looking like this."

She slid her arms into the oversized shirt and buttoned it up, not protesting when he left the kitchen. Her hands were shaking and coated in blood. Her earlier thought of wanting to lap it up had her running to the sink and washing her hands, nausea hitting her. She breathed through her mouth, trying not to throw up. The water continued to run and she held her hands under it, blood swirling around in the sink. She'd attacked a man. Sliced across his stomach so his blood had run over her claws.

Leaning forward, her forearms resting on the kitchen bench, she closed her eyes. It didn't help. She saw the blood flow again. At the time she'd felt the satisfaction she normally felt at besting someone in a fight. Rarely was there blood. A few busted lips, a handful of nose bleeds. Occasionally they'd been hers or Nate's.

"Claire?"

She spun to face Roy, surprised to find him so close. She stepped to the side and away from him, her gaze drawn to his side that was stained with blood. "How bad is it?"

"It's stopped bleeding already. Barely a graze." He

turned off the tap. "We have to go. I found a vehicle we can use."

She nodded, wrapping her arms around herself. "Where are we going?"

"I'll let you know when we get there."

She followed him through the house and into a garage, the roller door open, a four-wheel-drive parked inside. Opening the passenger door, she saw the gun Roy had held on Stanley earlier and a dagger. She stared at them, frozen in place. They were between the two seats, sitting in the open centre console, the handles of both protruding past the otherwise empty compartment.

"Get in the vehicle." Roy climbed in the driver's seat, adding the other two daggers to the collection and tossing the torn clothes onto the back seat. His tone softened. "Claire, they could return at any minute. Wayne, Stanley and any number of Knight Mages. They can travel to places instantly."

Visions of men appearing out of nowhere had her climbing into the vehicle and closing the door, automatically buckling up. "Where are we going?"

"I need to contact my family." Roy glanced down at his body before he checked over his shoulder and started the vehicle, reversing onto the road.

"We're going to your home?"

Roy shook his head. "Someone might be watching my place. And we can't take this vehicle there. It probably has some kind of tracking device. We'll keep moving until it's dark and then ditch it."

"What about the weapons? We can't walk around the streets with a gun and daggers." She had visions of being carted away in a police car. When she started talking about mice and dragons they'd probably head for the nearest hospital.

"We'll figure something out." He glanced at her. "Are you okay?"

She stared at her hands, seeing blood even though she'd washed it off. What was that Shakespearean play they'd read at school where the woman couldn't get the blood off her hands? She felt like washing them again. "I don't think so." She looked at Roy. "Will he die? Tobiah. Will he die?" Was she too old to burst into tears and cry for her dad? Right now that felt like a distinct possibility. She'd even be happy to see her mum and listen to a list of her many shortcomings.

"Knights tend to regularly be injured in battle. You surprised them. They were expecting a Dragon Mage and you turned into a dragon instead."

Her gaze remained on her hands. "How is that possible?"

"I don't know."

His words drew her gaze to him. "What do you mean you don't know? You turned into one so you must know how it's possible."

"I can't turn into anything other than a dragon. You can also turn into a mouse so you have to be a Dragon Mage. But then you shouldn't be able to turn into a dragon."

"None of what you're saying makes sense. Didn't you talk about Knight Mages earlier? What's a Dragon Mage?" She closed her eyes, trying to think of anything other than blood coating her claws. Her claws! The words made her want to scream. Was it too late to start screaming? Or fall apart.

"Dragon Mages are with the dragons and Knight Mages are with the Knights. Although things aren't that simple anymore. Not since the arrival of Hell Hounds. Not that they were overly simple before."

If she spent one more second thinking about dragons and Knights she might fall apart. "I need to find Bub, my mum's dog. I'm supposed to be looking after him."

"As soon as it's dark I'll ring my mum and ask her to look for him."

Claire hesitated. "He comes to the name Bubbles."

Roy grinned. "Who named him?"

"It wasn't me. My mum is hopeless at coming up with names."

"Who chose yours?"

"Mum."

Roy glanced at her. "Lucky she gets it right sometimes."

She stared at him. Had that been a compliment? "You like my name?"

Roy glanced at her again. "Yeah. Don't you?"

"Not particularly. Why do you like it?" And why was she having a normal conversation when her world was falling apart and the impossible was supposedly possible? No, she wasn't going to think about that. At least for a few minutes while she tried to keep herself from falling apart.

"It's not some fancy name that belongs to a girl who'd fall apart and burst into tears at the first sign of trouble. It has a sound of strength to it."

It was a good thing she hadn't burst into tears and called for her dad. She wasn't as strong as he thought, but she wasn't about to ruin his impression. "What's wrong with the fancy type?"

"I'm a Knight."

"You do know that doesn't explain anything to me."

He pulled up at a red light, his gaze drawn to her.

"I value strength, honesty and integrity. Above all, loyalty."

A shiver went through her at the look he gave her. "Loyalty."

He gave a single nod, reaching out to touch her hand. "You fought at my side. I didn't expect that." He glanced at the lights. "My oath was freely given. I didn't expect anything in return. You were drawn into this situation through no fault of your own." He held her gaze for another second before facing forward, driving off when the lights changed.

Chapter Five

Claire stared at Roy. The darkness of his skin, which made the blood harder to see, the well-defined muscles and the broadness of his chest. He fought like a warrior and yet she'd also seen gentleness. Her gaze was momentarily drawn to her injured hand. Had experienced it. Her gaze returned to Roy. "What is happening?"

"You'll need to be a little more specific."

"Why were you kidnapped? Who is Amber and why would she exchange herself for you? Why shouldn't I be able to turn into both a mouse and a dragon and since I can, what does that make me? Dragon Mage? Knight Mage? What is going on? Tell me everything." And did he like more than her name and that she'd fought at his side? She pushed that question aside. It shouldn't be important. Normally she would ask, but there were other things to focus on. She frowned. "Why do we seem to be driving around in circles?"

"I can't answer all of your questions. I don't know the answers."

"Which ones can't you answer?" It better not be about what she was.

"I don't know what you are."

"That wasn't what I wanted to hear. You're a dragon. And a Knight. Or so you say. You must know."

"We're driving around in circles so I can get to know the area of the house we were kept in. It isn't one belonging to the Queensland branch of Knights. Although we are in Brisbane where we have our headquarters."

She swallowed hard at his reply. "Queensland branch? There are more?"

"It's a worldwide organisation."

She closed her eyes, tilting her head back. What had she got herself mixed up in? "Drop me off somewhere." Opening her eyes, she faced him. "I'll find my own way home."

"Dressed in a shirt that looks like it belongs to a boyfriend, with bruises forming on your face and legs, blood spray in your hair and on your face. I can smell the metallic scent of it from here."

"I can't smell anything." She tried to ignore the other words he'd spoken, but the image they conjured wasn't a pretty one. "I feel like I'm coming down with a cold or something. And my ears are blocked again and won't pop." She yawned in the hope that would work. They remained blocked.

"What about when you're an animal?"

"Which one?"

Roy grinned. "Either."

Her gaze remained on his mouth for a moment before she forced it upwards. He really needed to stop grinning. It was highly distracting. "Yeah."

"Yeah isn't an answer to a multiple choice question. Can you smell or hear better when you are one of your animals and if so, which one?"

"Yes and both." She looked out of the window. "There's an hour or more until it's dark." Surely they couldn't randomly drive around until then.

"There must be something wrong. You should be able to smell and hear better while you're human. And see better too."

"I feel like I'm coming down with something."

"Amber might–" He broke off.

"Amber might what?"

Roy slowed to turn a corner, waiting until he'd sped up again before he spoke. "They might be expecting that. This was all to get to her. If she came to Brisbane, they might be able to kill her."

"She doesn't need to come here. All she needs to do is answer some questions about what I am."

Roy glanced at her. "You don't know Amber."

"I don't know anything," she muttered. And it was really starting to annoy her. A growl rose and she pressed her hands against her mouth. She didn't know if she should be horrified or relieved it hadn't been a squeak. "I want to get rid of this. I want everything back to normal." There hadn't been anything wrong with her life the way it had been. It had suited her just the way it was.

"Life doesn't work like that."

She faced him, trying to figure out the meaning behind his words. There'd been a bitterness she hadn't heard before. "What does that mean?"

"No matter how much you might wish otherwise you can't change what you've become. You will always have the ability to become a dragon."

A frown formed as she continued to stare at him. "You don't like it either."

"I shouldn't be one. I'm a Knight."

"You keep saying that like it should mean something to me."

"Were you read fairytales as a kid?" He glanced at her when she remained silent. "I guess you were."

"Knights kill dragons."

"Yes."

She wrapped her arms around herself, trying to hold herself together. She wasn't about to fall apart now. Not after facing a gun, three kidnappers, vanishing men and a dragon. Words shouldn't make her feel like she wanted to run screaming. "Are there many… dragons?" She'd tried to ask how many Knights, but her courage had failed in a big way and she'd barely managed to speak the word 'dragons'. So much for having a strong sounding name. But she'd never faced anything like this before. Schoolyard bullies were nothing compared to having a gun pointed at her.

Roy didn't answer immediately. "There are countless dragons."

She had no idea if that was good or bad. A thought occurred to her and she felt like an idiot. "What if you drop me at my mum's house?" She knew where the key was hidden.

"Looking like that?"

"No one is there. I can get-" A wry smile formed. "Actually, I can't get you anything to wear. My stepdad's shirts would be too small for you." She looked down at the shirt she wore. "And this one is stained with blood."

Roy was silent for a moment. "That might work. I won't be able to pull up for long. You get changed, grab some wet cloths for me and a cap, probably a cap for you too, and I'll pick you up in twenty minutes."

For a moment she almost told him to forget it. This was his problem, not hers. He could keep driving and never come near her again. Her ears popped for a split second and sound rushed in on her, causing her to wince. She was glad when they became blocked again.

"What's wrong?"

"How do you cope with increased hearing? And what about smell? I can't imagine a city smells all that good."

"You learn to turn them down."

"Like a stereo?" She didn't bother keeping the scepticism from her voice. Did he think she was an idiot? No one came with a dial and there were plenty of people she wished had one. And she was pretty sure there was more than a handful who'd had that thought about her over the years.

"What suburb are we heading to?"

She gave the full address, not just the suburb, before demanding, "Turn it down like with a dial?"

"It's the easiest way to explain it. Not that it's a physical object, more like a mental ability." He shrugged. "Isa-" He broke off, starting again almost instantly. "Others are better at explaining this sort of stuff."

Had he been about to say Isaac? That was the name Amos had mentioned when they'd spoken together in his backyard. "How many are you protecting? The ones you said would be at risk if those guys learned what you are."

He glanced at her, not answering, remaining silent for almost a minute. "How are you feeling? You seem calm."

"Yeah well, you're not in my head," she said dryly.

"I try not to be without asking."

"You try... what?" Shock raced through her. He couldn't have said that. Surely not.

"Be in your head. It annoys me when others do that. Thoughts are meant to be private."

It took her a few seconds to be able to form a coherent sentence. "You can read minds." She didn't care about the accusation she could hear in her tone and that Roy would have to have been deaf not to notice. He'd already shown he was anything but deaf.

"Not exactly. I'm not as good as a dragon."

"But you are a dragon. I saw you."

"Only one of my parents is a dragon. And not a full dragon at that. At the most I'm a quarter dragon."

She lowered her head into her hands. How had life become so complicated and out of control? She raised her head. "What day is it?"

"Saturday."

"How do you know?"

A grin momentarily appeared. "Because I'm only hungry, not starving."

That made sense. "What are we going to do?"

"About?"

She lifted her hands a fraction, palms up, spread wide. Did he really want a list? "I don't know. Everything?"

"You need to figure out what you want to deal with if you hope to come up with a workable plan."

"Did you read that in a book?"

"My uncle taught me."

"Oh." What sort of uncle taught his nephew that? She felt laughter bubble up and managed to force it away. Harold from over the road might actually be right. Did being a Knight count as being in a gang? "Was there a shoot up at your house earlier this year?"

Roy glanced at her, a startled expression crossing his face. "Who told you?"

"Harold. He said your family are in a gang."

"That sounds like Harold."

"Was there?"

"Yeah."

"Does that mean the old lady at the end of the street is actually a drug dealer?"

Roy chuckled. "She takes in ironing." He pulled up. "Be ready in twenty."

Checking out the window, Claire was surprised to see she was in front of her mum's house. "Okay." With a glance towards the daggers and gun, she opened the door and clambered out of the vehicle. A look around showed the street was empty and she ran towards the house, not wanting anyone to see her. She winced when she stood on the sharp bits of gravel scattered across the concrete driveway. As far as she knew there were no nosey neighbours that spent their time making up rumours, but she didn't want to take the chance.

The key was under a pot plant on the far side of the verandah that ran across the front of the house. The cold metal felt oddly comforting after the day she'd had. A glance towards the sky showed there was very little of the day left. Night would fall soon and then Roy could contact his family. Stepping inside the house she tried not to think about what that meant. Would his uncle be there? The one who'd taught him about making plans. Were the rest of them Knights? She had so many questions and no one to answer them. Not even Roy had been helpful. He'd ignored most of her questions and mainly commented on the ones that weren't answerable. She wasn't going to let him get away with that when she saw him in twenty minutes.

Chapter Six

Striding to her room, Claire grabbed jeans and a long sleeved shirt before having a quick shower. Once she was dressed, she found a plastic bag and wet some rags, she hoped her mum wouldn't miss, and put them in the bag. It, along with a packet of biscuits and a bottle of water went into a cloth backpack. She jammed the bloody shirt in too and grabbed an old jacket, a pair of sneakers and a couple of caps before she headed outside to wait for Roy. After slipping the key back under the pot plant, she waited on the footpath, walking to the edge of the road when he pulled up.

"You didn't have any problems?"

"No." She handed him a cap, the other one on her head. "If you want to stop somewhere we can swap places and you can get cleaned up."

"You can drive?"

"I have my Ps. But not having P plates isn't a problem since you're obviously driving around without them. I doubt you're old enough to have your opens."

"Eighteen."

She'd been right. He was only a year older than her. "How did you learn to fight like you do when you're so young?"

"My family are Knights."

"You're really going to have to stop doing that."

"Doing what?"

"Acting like saying the word 'knights' answers all questions. It doesn't."

Roy chuckled. "If you think about it, then it does." He pulled up onto the side of the road and got out of the vehicle to walk around to the passenger side.

Claire clambered over to the driver's seat, pulling the door closed that Roy had left open slightly. She waited until he was seated before she spoke. "Are you saying you were born with a sword in your hand? That unlike the rest of us you were teething on blades and learned to fight instead of crawl." She gestured towards the backpack she'd left on the passenger side floor. "Wet rags are in there."

Roy rummaged around in the backpack, holding up the packet of biscuits. "When are these for?"

"When we ditch the vehicle. I thought it'd be mean to eat in front of you and the last thing we need is to be pulled over by the cops for eating while driving. You've got a gun and three daggers in here."

Roy returned the food to the backpack and took out the plastic bag of wet rags, using them to clean the blood from his body. "I learned to walk before I could fight. You really need to be able to stand upright first."

She smiled at the humour in his voice. "Does that bother you?"

"No. Never. I'm a Knight."

She laughed softly. "Okay, it fits this time. But it isn't always the right answer." Shock ran through her. How could she be calm enough to drive through streets that were becoming crowded by more cars and have a conversation with someone who technically was a stranger?

"Are you okay?" Roy returned the rags to the plastic bag before putting the bag into the backpack. He wrapped the weapons with the torn clothes before slipping them into the backpack too.

"Why did you ask that?"

"Your heart rate increased and your breathing became uneven."

His words made her try and keep her breathing

even when she'd have preferred to pull over and tell him to stop. Everything. She didn't want to be a dragon and certainly didn't want to be a mouse. She wasn't the slightest bit like a mouse. Why would she be able to turn into one? "Why a mouse?"

"The droppings on the floor in the cell."

"And being able to turn into a dragon?"

"I don't know. Only those who are born that way are meant to be able to turn into one. I thought you might have dragon ancestors, but discarded that idea."

"Why?"

"Because dragons can't become mages. Either types of mages."

"How do you know I'm a mage?" She slowly shook her head. "My life sounds like an RPG."

Roy chuckled. "Wait until you see Hell Hounds. Then you'll feel like your life has become an RPG." He pointed to a parking spot up the road. "Pull over there."

She did as he said, not wanting to ask about Hell Hounds. She had a feeling they were as bad as they sounded. She didn't want her life to become a role playing game. "Where are we going?"

"For a walk. There's a phone box a few blocks from here. Can you go that far?"

She frowned as she got out of the vehicle, her

frown deepening when she saw Roy wipe over all the surfaces they'd touched. She waited until he was beside her, the backpack slung over one of his shoulders, and they were striding down the road. "Why did you wipe everything over?"

"Fingerprints."

His answer left her with other questions, but she supposed he'd at least said something other than 'knight'. "The police will be involved?"

"No, but some Knights aren't as honourable as others and aren't above checking law enforcement databases illegally. I didn't know if your prints would be in any system."

"Do I look like a criminal to you?"

"Do I look like a Knight to you?"

She was about to say no. "Yeah, actually, you do. Or at least a warrior, which is pretty much the same thing." When he smiled, she glared at him. "Does that mean I look like a criminal?"

"No. Most people think shining armour when knights are mentioned. I was expecting you to say no."

Not knowing what to say, she remained silent, trying not to think too hard about everything. Her day had been a disaster. So much for telling her dad she could take care of herself. Her breath caught at the thought of him and she wanted to ring up and demand that he come home. But he wouldn't be back for two weeks. The time felt like it would take forever. Normally it seemed to go by in a rush.

Roy reached out and took hold of her hand. "My family will be here soon. They'll help us figure out what to do."

"Don't Knights kill dragons?"

"Not all Knights. I have a few friends who are dragons and a few who are Dragon Mages." He paused a moment. "I've also got enemies who are dragons and ones who are Knights and Knight Mages."

Startled, she looked at him. "You're only eighteen. How can you have enemies? I thought the ones who captured you were after someone called Amber, not you."

"Amber turned eighteen last month. I was eighteen on the twenty-first of March. She's younger than me."

"Are you kidding me?" She winced at how loud her voice was, glancing around at the people who were on the footpath. No one looked at them. Didn't even glance their way. The streetlights lining the side of the road clearly showed they weren't the slightest bit interested. "How can someone have enemies when they're that young?"

"It's a long story. Anything involving a dragon tends to be a long story."

"She's a dragon?"

"A Dragon Mage."

"I hope you realise I'm more confused now than I was before you started to explain things."

Roy smiled fleetingly. "Sorry."

She eyed him. He hadn't sounded sorry. Amused more than anything else.

"We're nearly there."

She looked ahead to see a phone box. Her steps slowed. "What happens next? What will your family do?" She felt her heart rate speed up, but could do nothing about it.

Roy squeezed her hand he continued to hold. "They'll help me protect you. I gave my oath."

Coming to a stop, she stared up at him. "Shining armour would suit you." Her gaze travelled over his bare chest. "Although it'd be a shame to hide all those muscles." She grinned at the startled look that crossed his face.

Roy glanced away for a moment. "We better ring my family. My mum is probably causing havoc and wanting to kill someone by now."

She walked beside him. "Why do I get the feeling you mean that literally?"

"I do."

There was nothing she could say to that. Who mentioned that their mother would kill someone in the same kind of tone that they'd use to say their mother drove them to school? An ordinary, everyday kind of fact. "Has she?" When he glanced at her, a question in his eyes, she said, "Killed someone."

"She's a Knight."

"I forgot. That explains everything." She glared at him when he grinned.

They reached the phone box and Roy made a reverse charge call. "I'm okay, Mum." He paused a moment.

Claire took a step closer to him, trying to hear what was said on the other end of the line. It was impossible. Her ears remained blocked.

"Wayne, Stanley and Tobiah." Again he paused. "I know." Another pause. "No, I've got no way of getting home and it's probably best I don't come home in case someone is watching the place. I also have someone with me." He smiled reassuringly at Claire as he listened. "All right. I'll do that. Don't go killing anyone innocent." He chuckled. "I will." He hung up the phone and faced Claire again. "We need to catch a taxi."

"Why? And how are we going to pay for it?" Her handbag was at home. Her dad's home, which was right next door to the house Roy said they had to avoid. And she doubted Roy would have needed to reverse phone call charges if he'd had any money on him.

"One of my uncles will meet us and pay for it." He took out the packet of biscuits and opened them, offering them to her first.

She took a handful, walking silently beside him, having no idea what she should say. It wasn't until they were walking towards a parked taxi, the biscuits all eaten and the water bottle empty, that she spoke. "What about me? What will I do?"

Roy took hold of her hand. "You're worried. You shouldn't be. I made you a promise."

His words didn't reassure her. He'd promised to protect her with his own life. There was nothing reassuring about someone needing to make an offer like that. "What are we going to do about Wayne, Stanley and Tobiah?"

"You don't need to do anything. I'll take care of them. With help from my family."

She stopped to face him before he could enter the

taxi. "You make it sound like everything will shortly be over for me, but it won't. You said I'll always be able to…" She glanced through the window at the taxi driver. "That the changes are permanent."

Roy squeezed her hand. "We'll sort everything out once we meet up with my uncle." He held her gaze a moment longer before he let go of her hand and opened the car door, gesturing for her to enter.

Once seated, she looked out the window at the well-lit street outside, traffic flowing past. She wanted to go home. She didn't need any other problems in her life. There were more than enough of them already.

The trip was silent and when the taxi arrived at their destination, Amos, the man she'd seen vanish from Roy's backyard early that morning, paid the driver. They stood on the footpath with him, not moving away until the taxi had driven off. Amos led them to a dark coloured four-wheel-drive.

Claire took a step backwards. "You know, I think I'll find my own way home." Amos came around the vehicle to join her on the footpath, his eyes the same colour as his nephew's. There the similarity ended. They didn't contain any of the compassion or humour she'd seen in Roy's eyes. She tensed, struggling not to take another step backwards.

Amos breathed in deeply. "You live next door to my sister."

"How do you know?"

"Your scent."

She did take a step back at that comment. "Like that's not a weird thing to say."

"No more weird than being able to scent dragon on you. That's new. So is the smell of rodent." Amos looked to Roy. "You have a lot of explaining to do." He held out a phone. "And call Eliza before she tears the house apart then goes hunting."

Roy took the phone, his gaze going to Claire. "You're safe. Uncle Amos won't hurt you." He paused a moment. "You can sit in the front if you want."

Chapter Seven

Claire looked between Roy and Amos. She was beginning to feel like she'd only be safe if she got in the car. Amos wouldn't accept her refusal and appeared to be the type of person willing to do anything to make her comply. Regardless of what Roy said. "I'll sit in the back." It would be further away from Amos. Although not far enough.

Once they were in the vehicle, Amos drove off, Roy on the phone to his mum, reassuring her once again. When he hung up, he handed the phone back to Amos. The rest of the drive was silent and they eventually arrived at an industrial shed, parking in front of chain wire gates.

Claire reached for the door handle, freezing when Amos reached between the front seats and grabbed hold of her arm, preventing her from moving. "Let me go." She met his dark eyes, refusing to show how afraid she was. A pity her racing heart had probably given her away.

"Don't run. I will chase after you. You're not to go anywhere until I have answers." Amos continued to hold her arm until she nodded.

She tried to convince herself that the only reason she'd agreed was that she wanted answers too. She turned to Roy, who opened the door for her. "Does that promise include everyone?" She half expected him to say he wouldn't go against his uncle to protect her.

"Yes." Roy held out a hand.

Ignoring it, she slid out of the vehicle, taking several steps forward when Roy stepped out of the way, pushing the door of the vehicle closed. "Let's get the questions over and done with." She wanted answers.

Roy watched her for a moment longer before he gave a single nod and led the way to the gates Amos had unlocked. He glanced over his shoulder before he stepped through.

Claire followed him, having no idea what she'd find. When Amos unlocked the door of the building, she stepped inside what looked like a small, modern, open living apartment. In front of her was a kitchenette, two stools set at a bench, past them was a lounge suite and a television on a cabinet with wheels. On the far wall were two doors. "Where do they lead?"

"The one on the left leads into the work shed, the one on the right is a bathroom." Amos strode to the kitchen, gesturing towards the stools. "Take a seat." He leaned back against the far kitchen bench, standing in the 'U' shaped area and facing towards the stools.

She remained standing. "I need to go home. I have to find my mum's dog."

"Is it an annoying little thing that looks like a wig belonging to a rag doll? Probably a possessed one."

A grin escaped at Amos' description. "Pretty much."

"Eliza found him. She's locked him in her bathroom. She was planning to take him to a local vet tomorrow and get him scanned for a microchip."

"He's okay?"

Amos shrugged. "If he keeps making that awful high pitched noise he won't be."

"My back door is unlocked. She can return him to my place if she wants."

"I'll let her know." He held her gaze a moment longer before he turned to Roy, who was seated on one of the stools. "Tell me what happened after I left.

Your parents ran outside to see what was going on, when the dog wouldn't shut up, only to see you taken away by someone they didn't recognise."

"That'd be Tobiah," Roy said.

Claire spoke at the same time. "The dog's name is Bubbles."

Amos didn't look in her direction, his gaze remaining on Roy. "Eliza said that whoever he is, she's going to cause him a great deal of pain for laying a hand on you."

Roy grinned. "Claire sliced him up. Bad enough Wayne had to rush him off for medical help."

Amos inclined his head. "Start from the beginning."

Claire listened as Roy told about being captured, waking up to see her with the Pliethin, him becoming a dragon and her turning into a mouse. He described the location of the house, the layout and described their escape, including how she'd become a dragon.

She wanted to take a step backwards when Amos' gaze shifted to her. Instead, she met his gaze, refusing to be intimidated. "What does it mean?"

Amos turned to Roy. "We keep this to ourselves. It might come in handy. We also need to figure out what she can do."

"I will tell Amber eventually."

Amos closed the distance between him and the bench, unable to come any closer to Roy. "She is not your friend. How many times do I have to tell you that?"

"She's not my enemy either." Roy smiled. "Or so she told me."

"That was ages ago. You know how quickly alliances change with dragons."

"Amber is human."

Claire looked between them, trying to follow the conversation. She doubted they'd answer any of the many questions she had.

"She hasn't been human for a long time. You can't trust her." Amos almost growled the words.

Roy rose from the stool, his gaze clashing with that of his uncle. "Then what's that say about us? How human are we?"

Silence hung between them, neither looking away.

Fearing there'd be a fight, Claire struggled to think of something to say. "When can I go home?"

"Tomorrow." Amos continued to stare at Roy.

"Where am I meant to stay until then?" Claire demanded.

"Here." Amos kept his gaze on Roy.

"There's no bed." She fought the urge to get

between them. Not that it would have helped. There was no space. Both stood close to the bench.

Amos finally looked away, making a sound of exasperation as he looked at Claire. "The lounge pulls out into a bed. There's food in the fridge and no one will be around here on the weekend." He faced Roy again. "You are not to tell the dragons any of this."

"I'll tell Amber once they're no longer after her. While she's at her castle, she's safe. They won't be able to get to her there."

Claire's mouth dropped open. Amber had a castle? She was only eighteen. How did one get a castle at eighteen?

Amos pointed a finger at Roy. "She might have you and Isaac fooled, but not me." He strode towards the door.

"You're going?" Claire followed him. "You're leaving us here?"

He stopped, his hand on the doorknob. "I'll be back tomorrow after I make sure no one is watching my sister's house. Or if they are, figure out what else we can do."

"How about figuring out a way to stop me from being a dragon. Or a mouse."

Amos lowered his hand. "The best I can do is teach you how to be a dragon. You're on your own when it comes to the mouse." He grabbed hold of her wrists, lifting her hands so they were palm up. "Keep them there."

She stopped trying to pull away from his grip, keeping her hands in place when he let go of her. When he placed his hands above hers, a few centimetres between them, she struggled to hold them in place and keep them open. A pulling feeling formed in her palm and flames flickered to life. Again her mouth dropped open. She stared at the ball of fire sitting on each palm. Warm yet not burning. "How is this possible?" Her stomach lurched and she regretted having eaten the biscuits. Any moment now they might come back up. She swallowed hard, lifting her gaze to meet Amos'. "What is going on?"

"You're a Dragon Mage that can turn into a dragon. It shouldn't be possible." Amos nodded to her hands. "Put that fire out and both of you stay inside. This place is lined so no one will be able to find you."

He was gone before Claire could ask him what he meant. The balls of fire remained in her hands. "How do I put these out?"

Roy shrugged. "Amber always closed her hands. It was like putting out a candle flame."

She took a deep breath, realising her sense of smell was working overtime and her hearing was improved. The sound of Roy's heartbeat was strong and steady. "You're not worried. Not even a little bit."

"I have concerns."

"Then why isn't your heart racing as rapidly as mine?" She closed her hands, surprised when the flames went out.

"You can hear it?"

She started to say yes, but her ears were blocked again and her smell was back to normal. "Not anymore." She frowned. "What is wrong with me?" Other than being able to turn into creatures and hold fire in her hands.

"Maybe the two different abilities are conflicting with each other. You can't be a dragon and a mage. Amber was certain of that."

"Then how am I?" She stared at him, waiting for an answer. None came. "Roy?"

The silence stretched out before he finally replied. "I don't know. All I can think is that it's something to do with a combination of everything. Dragon blood, dragon bone and the caged Pliethin."

She felt like striking out at someone and the only person around was Roy. She turned her back on him. It wasn't his fault. Not really. She drew in a shaky breath. "I'm going home tomorrow. I don't care what you have to do so I can, but I'm not staying locked away in here. It isn't much better than the cell we escaped from."

"Okay."

She spun to face him, surprised he'd agreed so easily. "I can?"

"They don't know who you are. As long as you keep a low profile, and probably wear a hat or something to make it hard to get a good look at your face, it should be okay. They really only want me."

"Then why can't I go home tonight?"

"They'll be more vigilant tonight. They know we'll need to go somewhere. They have no idea how injured I am and neither of us were dressed in clothes suitable for wandering the streets. The first place they'll think of is my home. Second they'll probably check the Knights' headquarters."

"So I can go home tomorrow."

"Yes."

She didn't feel the relief she'd expected to feel. "What did Amos mean by this place is lined?"

"A special stone so that no one can stay in the Void and no one can mentally see inside this area of the building."

"What is the Void?"

"Like another dimension that is between worlds

and used to travel between and across them. Some have the ability to remain in the Void for varying amounts of time and observe the place they have left or are about to enter."

A shudder went through her. It sounded creepy. She was never going to be able to get undressed without feeling like some voyeur was watching her. "How come no one else knows about all of this? There are dragons. Not exactly something that's easy to hide." Even if they weren't as large as she would have expected them to be.

A wry smile appeared. "Dragons tend to deal with those who find out information they shouldn't. Knights try and kill any dragon they discover and Hell Hounds want to kill everything. That doesn't leave many people to share the news. Those who are smart keep it quiet. After all, who would believe them?"

Chapter Eight

If it hadn't been for Roy's smile, Claire would have thought it a threat. Exhaustion washed over her. It had been a long day. "I'm tired."

"Do you want something to eat?"

She shook her head. Her stomach felt queasy and it was difficult enough keeping the biscuits down. She wanted to go to sleep and hope that when she woke up it was to find that everything had been a nightmare and wasn't true. But then that would mean she hadn't met Roy. "I want to go to bed."

He crossed the room, wheeling the television cabinet out of the way before unfolding the sofa bed. He took pillows from a nearby cupboard, the bed already made. "Do you need anything else?" He tossed the pillows onto the bed. "There are new toothbrushes in the bathroom vanity."

"Thanks." It didn't take her long to use the

bathroom and climb into bed. While she'd been in the bathroom, Roy had turned the overhead light off and a table lamp was now on. It cast a soft glow across the room. "Where will you sleep?" She pulled the bed linen up, lying down as she spoke.

"I can sleep on top of the blankets or on the floor. Your choice."

She stared at him, trying to figure out what he was thinking. He looked tired. Actually, more than tired. Fatigued and ill. "You can sleep on the blankets."

With a single nod, he strode to the bathroom, closing the door.

Lying there, she heard the shower start. For a second she wondered if it was because her hearing had improved, then realised it was because of the flimsy door between them. Closing her eyes, she waited for him to return to the living room. Before he did, she fell asleep, not a single dream disturbing her.

She slowly woke, frowning when she realised she wasn't in her own bed. The previous day came back in a rush and she tensed, turning her head to see Roy lay beside her.

He sat up, a dagger in his hand. "What is wrong?"

"You slept with that?" She couldn't take her gaze off the dagger.

"It was beneath the mattress." He glanced around. "Are you okay?"

"It wasn't a dream. Everything is real. I barely moved. What woke you?"

"Your heartbeat." Roy dropped the dagger onto the floor beside the sofa bed, grinning. "Do you want breakfast?"

"What are you smiling about?"

"There's been a few times I've had that exact thought. It never is a dream." His grin faded. "It doesn't have to change anything. Not if you don't want it to."

"What do you mean?"

"Amos can teach you about being a dragon. I can teach you how to fight." He smiled fleetingly. "I've had a lot of good teachers, including Rian, the son of one of the oldest dragons."

"Why would I need to learn how to fight if it doesn't have to change anything?"

"Because wyverns and dragons will know you're a dragon. If you stay out of deserted areas the wyverns won't be a problem and most dragons won't care about you if you do nothing to annoy them. But just in case, it's good to be prepared."

"I've been to self-defence classes on and off for years."

"This isn't about defence. It's about offence."

"I already get into enough trouble at school for fighting."

"Do you always win?"

Not as often as she'd like. "Sometimes." She shrugged. "They aren't always fair fights." Four against one had been the worst. Luckily Nate had arrived before she'd been beaten to a pulp.

"With the right training they could become fair." He paused a moment. "Why do you get into trouble for fighting at school?"

"Because I'm not good at walking away. Sometimes you shouldn't walk away."

"Like when?"

Like far too many times when she'd got into a fight she wasn't in the slightest bit able to handle because the one already in the fight was less skilled than her. She smiled, figuring out how to explain it to him. "You're a Knight. Shouldn't you already know which fights you shouldn't walk away from?"

Roy chuckled. "Didn't you tell me that wasn't an explanation?"

"Doesn't stop you from using it." She glanced past him to the kitchenette. "What happened to breakfast?"

The day passed slowly. Claire spent a lot of time

pacing the floor and watching the start of some of the many movies in the cabinet beneath the television. About the only thing she enjoyed was the lesson Roy gave her in fighting, having first pushed the furniture to the edges of the room. Afterwards, she returned to pacing while Roy made lunch.

Amos turned up after they'd eaten, a dagger in Roy's hand the moment the door handle had turned. He put it on the kitchen bench beside him once Amos entered the room, closing the door.

Amos gave Roy an approving nod before turning to Claire. "I can take you home now. It might shut that infernal dog up."

Claire grinned. "I doubt it."

"Why would you want a dog like that?"

She shrugged. "You'd have to ask my mum."

"There's been no one home."

"That's my dad's house. Mum and her new husband have gone to Europe for a month long holiday. I got to look after Bub."

"Sounds like you got the short straw," Amos said.

"Actually, I think I got the better bargain. Putting up with Bub is preferable to putting up with Bentley."

"Is that really his name?" Roy asked.

Claire chuckled when she looked over at him and saw his expression. "Too fancy a name?"

Roy nodded.

Amos spoke before Claire could make another comment about fancy names. "We have to go outside. I can't enter the Void from this room." He turned to Roy. "You need to stay here a bit longer."

"Why can't we go to my house the normal way?" Claire demanded.

"It's safest through the Void," Amos said. "You don't want to be seen with any of us."

Roy crossed the room and held out a torn off piece of paper.

Claire took it, glancing at the notepad and pen now on the kitchen bench. "What is it?"

"Try opening it and having a look," Amos said dryly.

"Phone number." Roy turned to Amos. "If you're going to leave me here can you bring my phone back? It's in my bedroom on my bedside cabinet."

Amos nodded, opening the door and gesturing outside. "I don't have all day."

She wanted to protest. Disappearing into some Void didn't sound safe. Looking towards Roy, she found no help. He nodded his head once. Not knowing where she was and how else she could get home, she stepped outside. Before she could tell Amos that he better not leave her in some Void, he grabbed her hand and the world around them became covered in a light fog for a second. She stepped out of the fog and into the laundry of her house.

"Stay inside." Amos was gone before she could say anything.

She stared at where he'd been, feeling disorientated, the sound of Bubbles barking in the background. Shaking her head, she checked the back door, locking it before looking for Bubbles. He was shut in the bathroom, leaves and twigs caught in his hair, a layer of dirt over everything. She sighed. "I think I'd rather face a gunman."

Bubbles growled before barking several more times.

"Yeah, well, look at you." She didn't mention the word bath. He would have really carried on then. But there was no other way she'd be able to get him clean.

After a couple of hours, Claire figured out the only way to get Bubbles clean was to trim his hair. By the time she was finished he looked about a quarter of his size and seemed to be glaring at her after the indignities she'd put him through.

"You were the one who got yourself in that state so don't go looking at me like that." She left him in the bathroom, the door open. A glance over her shoulder showed he wasn't following, more than likely sulking. He'd probably have his revenge. She closed the bedroom doors. Hers, her dad's and the spare room that was filled with unpacked boxes. At least that would reduce the amount of things he could chew up.

Reaching the kitchen, she saw her phone on the table where she'd left it yesterday morning. It seemed a lot longer than that. Drawing out the scrap of paper she'd pushed into her pocket, before dealing with Bubbles, she entered Roy's number into her phone. Her fingers hovered over the screen for a moment, finally deciding to send him a text to see how he was. Her phone rang. She stared at his name on the screen before she answered. "Is something wrong?"

"No. I wanted to make sure you were okay. I should have asked you earlier. How is your hand?"

She stared at it, having forgotten about it. "It's healed. Only a faint scar."

"Dragons heal quicker than humans."

She dropped into a nearby chair, nearly missing it. "I'm not-" She broke off, unable to argue his comment. Closing her eyes she tried not to see the image of her blood coated claws. "I am human."

"I didn't mean that you weren't. It's…" Roy trailed off. "Your dog was okay?"

"I had to clip him. And he's not my dog. I'd want one a lot better than that ex-mop."

"What sort of dog would you want?"

"I don't know. A bigger one. Large enough I wouldn't have to bend to pat it." She smiled when Roy mentioned a few larger breeds and they continued to talk about dogs, eventually going on to other topics. By the time she got off the phone, it was past bedtime and she made herself a sandwich, checking her emails while she ate it. Most of them she ignored. The only one she answered was from her dad. Her reply was short and each word a lie. Everything was not fine. She stared at her hand, trying not to see the image of claws. It didn't help. Turning off her laptop, she finished eating then got ready for bed, not wanting to be too tired at school the next day. No one should enter a battlefield half asleep.

Surprisingly, she had another dreamless night. Not that she dreamt often, but she'd expected something after all she'd gone through. As was becoming normal, Bubbles woke her before her alarm and she let him out the back door, shivering as she waited for him to finish up outside. When he started to head towards the fence, she ran after him, scooping him up before he could get away. She looked back at the door. How had she crossed that distance so fast? He should have been able to get away. He was a lot faster than her.

Her steps were slow as she returned inside. She was human. Closing the door she let Bubbles go. "I'm human."

He looked up at her and barked.

"Don't argue with me." She glared at him.

Wagging his tail, he rolled over so she could pat his stomach.

She rubbed her foot across it, sighing heavily. "I'm talking to a dog. How crazy is that?" Her phone rang, startling her. She shrank back, the world becoming large, folds of material dropping over her.

Bubbles barked excitedly, sniffing the garments on the floor, scratching at them enthusiastically.

Chapter Nine

Squeaking, Claire scampered towards her room, not reaching it before Bubbles pounced on her. She bit his paw and he drew back with a yelp, pausing in his chase. She scurried away, slipping under the door seconds before Bubbles ran into it. Facing the door, she huddled there quivering, the dog scratching and whining at the timber. Her phone, that had stopped ringing, began again.

This was ridiculous. She couldn't keep changing like this. Staring at her paw, she tried to stretch out, wanting to grow large again. Nothing happened. Glancing around the room, she spotted the mirror of her dressing table. It took a few minutes to figure out how to clamber up so she could see her reflection.

A brown mouse stared back at her from the mirror, large pink ears, black eyes and quivering whiskers. The phone began to ring again and she stumbled backwards at the sound, slipping on the surface and falling over the edge.

Her squeak turned into a shriek then she collided with the floor, the wind knocked from her lungs. Her human lungs. She lay there for a few seconds, the cold forcing her to her feet, and dragged out her school uniform. Once she was dressed, she opened the door, Bubbles still sniffing around the area looking for the mouse.

"Bad dog."

He barked before racing back to the pile of clothes, sniffing at them again.

She followed him slowly, scooping them up off the floor. The day wasn't off to a good start. She'd been woken before her alarm, nearly killed by a dog that technically wasn't big enough to hurt more than a fly, or a mouse, and tumbled off what had started out to be the size of a cliff. Would it have killed her if she'd hit the floor as a mouse? She didn't want to know.

The phone began to ring again and she dumped her clothes in her room before she answered it. "Roy."

"Are you okay?"

"I had a bit of a rodent problem."

Roy chuckled.

"It's not funny. The stupid dog nearly killed me."

"I'm sorry."

"Was there a reason you rang so early?"

"I wanted to check on you."

"So you rang early." She headed to the kitchen and began preparing her school lunch.

"Bubbles always wakes you early. I hear him around this time every morning."

"I didn't realise he was so loud."

"He is a bit, but I've also got good hearing."

"Oh. Right."

"I try not to eavesdrop on people, but some sounds are hard to ignore. Anyway, I wanted to tell you to call me any time you need help. No matter the hour."

"Okay."

"I'll talk to you later."

She started to say goodbye. "Wait. How are you?"

"Bored."

She heard the humour in his voice and smiled. "Tell your uncle he needs better movies."

Roy laughed softly. "I'll let you finish getting ready for school."

"Okay. I'll talk to you later." She was still smiling and thinking back over their conversation by the time she was heading out the door, a cap pulled down low. He'd taken note of the fact Bubbles woke her up early. Did that mean he'd noticed her too? She didn't know. There was obviously only one way to find out.

Unlocking her car, she threw her schoolbag on the back seat before she got in, worried about how she'd get through a day at school without turning into a mouse or dragon.

The day began as it always did. Arriving just in time, scrambling to get to her seat before her teacher complained that she was late. She sat beside Nate, shrugging when he asked how her weekend had been. Nate stopped talking when the teacher glared at him for a few seconds, his lips barely moving when he said he'd meet her at lunch.

Her classes were the same as always. Nothing happened to make her turn into a mouse or dragon and she began to think she'd worried for no reason. When the bell rang for lunch she nearly bolted from her chair, starving. It didn't take her long to eat her lunch as she walked towards where she usually met up with Nate. She tried to sidestep the figure that deliberately stepped in front of her, but there were other students in the way.

"Watch it," Turquoise snarled. She was slim and tiny, blond hair swept back from her face that had a light application of makeup.

"You were the one to walk in front of me. Maybe you should watch where you're going." Her hands went to her hips and she glared at Turquoise. There was no way she was going to wear the blame.

"How dare you talk to me like that?"

Claire grinned. "I'll talk to you however I want." Spotting Linden striding towards them, she struggled to keep her smile in place. She should have known Turquoise's boyfriend wouldn't be far away. Everything would be fine if none of his mates turned up. She could handle Linden.

"Apologise," Turquoise demanded.

"Make me." The words were automatic. She couldn't have prevented them even if she'd tried. There was no way she'd apologise for something she hadn't done.

Linden stopped at Turquoise's side. "You sure about that?"

Even though he was easily as tall and broad as Roy, she didn't back down. "She should apologise to me." She curled her hands into fists, letting them hang loosely at her sides, watching him carefully.

"You should apologise for being in the same town as us." Linden grinned. "No, make that for being born."

"Like I haven't heard that before. How original." She saw his movement before he had a chance to get close, stepping to the side and striking out before she was behind him.

Linden spun to face her, his longer arms nearly connecting before she could get out of the way. "Wouldn't want to say anything too original. It'd take you too long to understand what I said."

She could feel the crowd gathering, people at her back. It felt uncomfortable. Her fist connected with his jaw and he staggered back, shock flaring in his eyes. She felt the same shock. Hadn't expected to hit him that hard, or move as quickly as she did. Scents and sounds burst in on her and she winced, trying to hold back the noise.

Linden shook his head, throwing himself at her with a growl.

She echoed the sound, scenting weak prey pressing in around her. She spun, her eyes narrowing as she spotted a scrawny looking kid. Movement had her spinning back to Linden, blocking his punch and sinking her fist into his stomach. Her skin crawled with an odd sensation.

"You're not going to hog all the fun, are you?"

Claire spun at the familiar voice, for a few seconds not recognising Nate. Sound and smell faded back to normal, her skin becoming familiar again as she stared at the tall, wiry, dark haired boy in front of her. "Nate."

His gaze was drawn to a point behind her and he took a step forward, opening his mouth to speak.

She spun before he could, again blocking Linden's fist, stepping in close to grab his other wrist and bend it back. "You would attack me from behind?" Her words were low.

"Don't blame me because you were distracted." Linden struggled to break free of her grip, wincing when she bent his wrist back further.

The word 'teacher' went through the crowd, a low hum that caused them to break off into groups.

Nate stepped close. "Time to go."

"They should apologise." She released Linden.

Nate slung an arm around her shoulders. "Forget about them. Come on." He tugged her to the side, striding with her to the spot where they normally hung out during lunch. "Who names their kid after a colour anyway? Turquoise. Might as well have named her orange or something."

"Then she'd be a fruit." She couldn't help thinking about Roy's comment on fancy names. Turquoise certainly wasn't a fighter. No, she had her boyfriend for that. Her boyfriend with the fancy name.

"Okay, green then."

Claire grinned. "That works. Certainly a colour and definitely not a fruit." Her grin faded. What would she have done if Nate hadn't joined her? She was pretty certain she'd been about to turn into a dragon before he'd distracted her. The other kids at school weren't her prey. The image of blood soaked claws flashed through her mind.

"What are you thinking about? You look serious all of a sudden."

Normally she could tell him anything. This wasn't something she could share. Roy had pretty much told her, in a roundabout way, that no one spoke about seeing dragons. She eyed Nate up and down. "I should have gone for a girl for a friend."

"Thanks." His tone was dry.

"You're welcome." She couldn't resist grinning. "How do you tell if a boy likes you?"

"You're right. You should have picked a girl."

"But how would they know? Shouldn't you know since you're a boy?"

He shrugged. "I guess they either tell you or show you."

"How do you know which sort they are?"

He shrugged again. "I don't know."

"What sort are you?"

A moment of panic crossed his face and he drew his

arm away from her shoulders. "The kind to tell. This isn't about me, is it?"

"Of course not." She screwed up her face. "That'd be like... I don't know. I can't think of anything bad enough to compare it to."

"That's a relief. You had me worried for a minute there." He paused a moment. "You're not planning on getting all girly and wanting to talk about some guy, are you?"

Laughter escaped. "You're the last person I'd talk to about that kind of thing." Not that she had anyone else she could talk to about it.

"Does he go to our school?" He glanced around.

"No."

"How did you meet him?"

"Thought you didn't want to hear this kind of stuff."

"Just the basics. Not the long looks, holding hands and sighs. You can keep all that kind of stuff to yourself."

She was tempted to ask him if he wanted to hear about gunfights, dragons, kidnappers and swords. "He's one of my new neighbours."

He grinned. "I'm guessing not the old lady who might be a drug dealer."

"No, the one Harold thinks might be in a gang and had a shoot out at his place at the start of the year."

"Is he?"

"He's not in a gang."

"But there was a shoot out at his place earlier this year?"

Chapter Ten

Claire stared at Nate for a moment, wishing she could tell someone about what was happening. Someone she trusted and knew would be on her side no matter what happened. "Something happened there earlier this year. But I don't know what exactly."

"You're not going to turn into one of those girls who chase after the bad boy, are you?"

"No." Could you call a Knight a bad boy? Weren't they meant to save the princess? An image of Roy holding two daggers came to mind, quickly followed by one of him with a gun. There'd been no shining armour involved, but there certainly had been dragons. Although she wasn't remotely like a princess and would be more likely to save herself than to wait around for some knight to come along and rescue her. "At least I don't think he is."

"Run for the hills. If you don't think he is, then he probably is."

She laughed. "If I should be running from anyone, it's you." She bumped his arm with her shoulder. "How many times have you led me into trouble?"

"How many times have you got me into trouble? I haven't got you into trouble anywhere near as often as you've led me astray." He hoisted himself onto the fence, leaning back against a broad tree that grew beside it, which had bent the metal bar that ran across the top of the fence.

"Not that many times." She perched on the fence beside him, leaning against the edge of the tree. "Move along. You're taking up all the space." She shifted along the fence when he did, so she was able to lean against more of the tree.

"You doing anything this weekend?"

Images of the past weekend flashed through her mind. "Not planning to. Why?"

"Can I crash at your place?"

She slowly shook her head. "Who is she?"

Nate grinned. "Someone I met yesterday. Can you imagine what it'd be like bringing her home to my place?"

Claire laughed. Nate had three younger brothers who always wanted to know everything he was doing and asked a million questions. Much younger brothers. "She'd be looking for an excuse to leave within minutes."

"Exactly. So can I?"

"The spare room is full of boxes that need unpacking."

"How about I help you sort them out this week after school."

"You must be really interested in her." She didn't bother hiding her grin.

"Come on, Claire. Is that a yes or no?"

She elbowed him. "Idiot. Of course it's yes."

His phone beeped and he took it out and checked his message, laughing. "You're a hit." He turned the phone so she could see the screen. "Dragon Lady."

She breathed in sharply as she stared at the image of herself, the words 'Dragon Lady' written across it. Either she had started to change or the blur of movement had made it seem like she might have claws and the dappled shadows of the nearby trees had given her skin a scaled appearance.

"Have you thought of a comeback yet? My favourite would have to be when they called you queen bitch and you agreed that you certainly did deserve a throne."

"You know I think I might let them use that

name." A smile slowly formed. Why was she so worried about what had happened? There was no reason she had to agree with Roy that being a dragon was terrible. "I've always liked dragons."

"You sound surprised."

"Not exactly surprised. I forgot it for a bit."

Nate turned the phone towards himself. "It's eerie. You could almost believe you were about to turn into a dragon."

"Send it to me." She wanted to show it to Roy. See if it was a trick of the light or if she'd actually started to change. "I can use it for my lock screen."

Nate chuckled, sending the image. "I think that's what Turquoise hates the most. No matter what she does to get under your skin it rolls straight off you. She can't get the reaction she's looking for. And fighting doesn't count. Everyone is convinced it's your favourite pastime."

"She obviously isn't trying hard enough." Not like Wayne, Stanley and Tobiah. They had got a reaction. She'd rather Turquoise didn't go to the same extreme. When the bell rang, she groaned. "I'm not ready for the afternoon classes."

Nate hopped off the fence. "Who is?" He walked beside her as they headed towards the school buildings. "How about I come over this afternoon and we can unpack some of the boxes."

"I do have homework to do."

"We can do that together. I'll help you with English and History and you can help me with Science and Maths." He slung an arm around her shoulders.

"Deal." And after that she'd talk to Roy about the picture. She sent him a text to let him know she needed to talk to him later that day.

"You texting the new guy?"

"His name is Roy."

"I don't care what he's called as long as he isn't like that one last year who kept trying to convince you fighting is bad. That's what I love most about you. You make sure we get in a fight at least once a day. Don't go letting anyone ruin that by changing you into someone you're not."

"I don't think Roy is the sort to complain about me getting into a fight." Not considering he slept with a dagger under the mattress.

"Talking of fights, there's a guy we need to teach a lesson to tomorrow."

"What did he do?" She didn't bother keeping the suspicion out of her voice. Nate liked to fight. If he'd ended up befriending anyone else he might have become a bully. Not one that picked on the younger kids, because he didn't think there was any challenge in that.

"He makes one of the kids in our class do his homework. He's not even paying him."

Her phone beeped to let her know she had a message. Checking it, she smiled.

"That smile is looking a little sappy."

"It is not." Poking her tongue out at Nate, she put her phone on silent and returned it to her pocket. "I'll meet you at my place after school." When he nodded, she parted company with him, leaving him at his classroom and heading to her own. Her smile returned. Roy would see her later today. She'd ask him how much later once school ended for the day. No point risking having her phone confiscated.

That afternoon when she pulled up at home, Nate had already arrived. Getting out of the car, her cap pulled down low, she pointed a warning finger at him. "If you lose your license I'm not going to be your chauffeur."

He pushed away from the door he leaned against. "Of course you would. I'd even let you drive my car."

She barely gave his car, which was parked on the footpath, a glance. "It's not that great a vehicle."

"Shh. You'll hurt her feelings." He blew his car a kiss.

She elbowed him as she passed him to unlock the door. "Idiot." The word was said fondly. She swung the door open, freezing when she saw Roy stood inside near one of the armchairs.

Nate pushed her inside, out of his way. "You must be Roy." He glanced at Claire and grinned. "The one who causes sappy smiles when he sends a text."

"It was not sappy." Her lips curved into a smile. "I have a long memory and I will tell your new friend all kinds of interesting stories this weekend." She took a step towards Roy. She hadn't expected him so soon. "This is Nate, my best friend."

Roy held out his hand to Nate. "You're right. I'm Roy."

Nate turned to Claire. "Does this mean I'm going to have to start ringing first in future?"

"I didn't realise you had plans this afternoon." Roy took a step backwards.

"It's okay," Nate said. "Best friend wasn't a euphemism for anything." He grinned. "And I'm not pining away for her either."

Roy looked from one to the other. "It looks like Claire isn't the only one who tends to have a habit of speaking bluntly."

"We've been friends since the start of high school. I always knew she'd be a bad influence on me," Nate said.

Claire snorted. "I'm not the one who's the bad influence." She faced Roy, trying not to smile. "But at least his name isn't fancy."

Roy shifted his weight to his other leg, glancing at Nate. "Uhm, well…"

"What am I missing?" Nate asked.

Claire grinned. "Roy doesn't like fancy names. They tend to go with fancy, useless people."

Nate chuckled. "He's met your stepdad."

"Actually, no. He hasn't met any of my parents."

"Interesting."

Claire hit Nate's arm with the back of her hand. "Watch it." She glanced towards the doorway. "Anyway, weren't you going to start unpacking those boxes? It's going to take time to unearth that room."

"I'm not doing it all by myself."

"Get started and I'll join you soon," Claire said.

Nate looked from Claire to Roy and back again. "Why didn't you say you wanted to greet him without an audience. It's not like you to beat around the bush." He strode from the lounge room before Claire could speak.

"Sorry." She smiled wryly. "He can be a bit much sometimes."

"Should I ask what you told him about me?" Roy closed the distance between them.

"Nearly nothing. He has a tendency to jump to conclusions."

Roy breathed in deeply. "Maybe, but I don't think he landed too far from the truth this time."

"Why did you say that?"

"Different emotions have different scents."

"I can't smell anything. And I want to be able to figure it out." She took out her phone and showed him the picture. "Is this a trick of the light and movement or was I starting to change?"

Roy frowned, enlarging the picture. "It might be a bit of both." He met her gaze. "You were in a fight today?"

Another wry smile made a brief appearance. "I'm in a fight nearly every day." She chuckled at the confusion that crossed Roy's face. "It's a long story. And involves Nate. That's how we met. First day of high school and I ended up in a fight with an older kid who thought I'd be an easy mark. Nate came along and asked if he could join in the fun." She shrugged. "And things snowballed from there."

"I was going to ask if you wanted me to start

training you this afternoon, but changed my mind when your friend arrived." He paused a moment. "I think I should change my mind again. And teach both of you."

"Why?"

"You need to learn how to fight without losing control. And as for Nate, the same reason I was lucky to be taught by Rian. You're only as strong as the weakest one you stand beside."

Now she was the one feeling confused. "Nate's not weak."

"I'm not talking strength. I'm talking skill. But I wouldn't want you to use what I taught you against those weaker than you." Roy continued to watch Claire, raising his voice. "Come in, Nate. No need to lurk in the hallway."

"What is going on?" Nate gestured towards the front of the house. "Is the old fellow right? Are you in a gang?"

"Harold," Claire said automatically.

"I'm not in a gang," Roy said.

"Then why would you want to teach us to fight like you're expecting some big battle or something?" Nate demanded.

"You never know what might happen," Roy said.

"Bullshit." Nate took a step closer to Roy. "You

know exactly why. Is Claire in trouble? What's going on?"

Chapter Eleven

Claire moved closer to Nate, resting her hand on his arm. "I'm not exactly sure where to start. Most of it isn't my story."

Nate faced Claire. "It's his?" He nodded towards Roy.

She let her breath out slowly, trying to push away the feeling that was similar to the one she'd felt when fighting Linden. Her hand tightened on Nate's arm, unable to grip it properly, struggling not to change forms. Her gaze was drawn to Roy. "What changed? You said I should be okay."

"I think Wayne and Stanley have more friends in Brisbane than I thought."

"What about Tobiah?"

"I looked through all the photos Uncle Amos took and he wasn't in a single one of them."

"What photos?"

"Of those watching my house and the other location."

Sound and smell rushed in on her and a growl escaped. They weren't going to kidnap her again. Either of them.

Roy was in front of her in a rush, grabbing her upper arms. "Focus."

Nate tried to drag Roy away from Claire. "Leave her alone." When Roy continued to hold on, Nate swung a fist towards him.

Roy ducked, pushing Claire behind him and raising his own fists.

"No!" She rushed forward, getting between them, rising above them to snarl at each of them.

Nate stumbled back, running into a wall and sliding down it. He attempted to speak several times.

Roy put himself between Nate and Claire. "You need to change back."

The protective feeling that had washed over her, faded. She shook her head. No way was she going to change back. She'd end up naked. Plucking at the shreds of her school uniform, she held a handful of them out to Roy. Her dad was going to be annoyed that she'd ruined another uniform. He'd think it was from fighting again.

"I'll get you a blanket." Roy retreated, grabbing

hold of Nate's arm and dragging him to his feet, tugging him towards the doorway.

Claire growled. She wasn't about to hurt Nate. He was her best friend. Stalking forward, she tried to communicate her thoughts. All she could do was growl again. A rumbling sound that filled the air around her.

"Is she still herself?" Nate asked.

"I don't know," Roy said.

She nodded her head, another frustrated growl escaping.

Roy stopped in the doorway, Nate behind him. "Are you calm, Claire?"

She pointed a claw at him. Barely managing not to growl when he took a step backwards, pushing Nate further into the hallway. Couldn't he understand she was as calm as him? Tilting her head to the side, she listened to his heart before tapping her own chest and pointing at him again. He wasn't as calm as usual. Had he really been worried about her hurting Nate? She'd never hurt him. Didn't he realise she was trying to protect them from each other?

Roy continued to face Claire. "Nate, grab a blanket for her."

"Why?"

"Because she'll be naked when she turns human."

"Serves her right for turning into a dragon and scaring the shit out of me," Nate said.

She gave him the middle finger, pleased with how much better it looked when given with claws.

Nate laughed. "She's good. I don't think she's going to slice us up or anything. Probably growling at us because we can't read her mind."

Claire pounced forward, nodding her head as well as tapping it. Anything had to be better than not being able to explain what was going on. Even having someone invade her mind.

Roy gave a single nod, while Nate asked what was going on. "*Can you hear me, Claire?*"

"*Yes. It feels odd. Can you hear me?*"

Roy spoke aloud. "Yes. Are you okay?"

"*Other than being stuck in this shape and having no idea how to get out of it.*"

"There's no point asking me. I don't know much about it. I don't… Saturday was… I just don't use that ability. I'll call Uncle Amos." Roy took out his phone.

Nate tried to push past Roy. "What's going on? Can you hear her? I feel like I'm listening to one side of a phone conversation."

"*Tell Nate to get the blanket off my bed. If I figure this out I don't want to be standing around naked again.*"

She growled when Roy answered his phone, turning away slightly and holding up a hand.

"Sounds like Claire is getting annoyed again," Nate said.

"*Roy!*"

He looked at her with a frown, continuing to explain the situation to his uncle and that they had another person with them. A friend of Claire's.

"*If you had sent him for a blanket I wouldn't have had to yell.*" She growled again.

Amos stepped out of the Void, causing Nate to jump backwards and swear. "What exactly is going on?"

"*How do I speak in his mind,*" Claire asked Roy.

"*He's here now,*" Roy's voice was again in her mind.

"*I need a blanket before I turn back. Not that I know how to do it.*"

Amos removed his shirt and tossed it to the side, wearing only a pair of leather trousers. "*Both of you pay attention. It's easier to show you exactly how it feels and what you should be doing than it is to explain.*" He turned to Nate. "Fetch a blanket."

"But I don't want to miss out on anything. I'm already missing out on most of the conversation." Nate raised his hand and took a step back when Amos took a single step towards him. "Okay, okay." He hurried out of sight.

A rumbling sound rose and Claire guessed it was her dragon version of a laugh. She really had to figure out what kind of look Amos had given Nate. It would come in handy.

"Both of you focus." This time Amos spoke aloud. Within a few seconds he'd turned into a dragon. A large ebony coloured dragon stood in front of Claire, gold flecks across his wings and in his hazel eyes. "*Did you follow what I did?*"

"That is so awesome." Nate came into the lounge room with a blanket he threw over Claire's shoulders. "Since the rest of the world doesn't know about dragons I guess this is one of those 'if you don't keep it I'm going to kill you' type of secrets."

Amos spun towards Nate, turning human in the same motion. "I will tear your heart out and feed it to dingoes."

Claire was between Amos and Nate, turning human without thinking. "You will not touch him."

Amos gave Roy a look of disgust. "You had to be drawn to one like Amber. We don't need any more hot headed people thinking only about their friends and family. This is bigger than that."

"Have you tried telling Mum that?" Roy grinned when Amos didn't answer. "I didn't think so."

Amos took a step back from Claire. "You need to practice changing forms without going into a panic about your friends."

She clutched the blanket around her, staring at Amos' legs. "I want a pair of those trousers." She pointed to Amos's legs. "And a top made from leather too."

"I want to be able to turn into a dragon," Nate said.

She stepped to the side so she could see Nate and keep an eye on Amos. "Apparently I'm a freak of nature and no one is meant to be able to turn into a dragon unless they're born one."

Nate started laughing.

Claire's eyes narrowed. "That better not be at me."

"Harold too. He's not even close to right. Now there's someone it'd be a pleasure to let him see the truth. Gangs!"

"Did you not understand what I said?" Amos' words were slow and menacing.

"He won't tell anyone." Claire stood between Nate and Amos again.

Nate stepped to her side, facing Amos. "As if I'd do anything that might hurt Claire."

Amos looked from Claire to Nate before turning

to Roy. "No." Both of them remained silent, meeting each other's gazes.

"They're talking in their heads, aren't they?" Nate asked.

"Whatever you're discussing, say it aloud. Don't leave us out of it," Claire said.

"It's none of your concern." Amos picked up his shirt. "I'll be back soon with clothes for the girl." He pointed a finger at Roy. "They are untrained and untrustworthy. We'll work something else out." He vanished from the room.

Nate took a step backwards. "That is the creepiest thing ever."

"It gets worse. They can remain in the Void and see out through a kind of light fog."

"I don't know whether to feel creeped out by that or ask if there are hot female dragons." Nate grinned. "You don't count."

Claire slowly shook her head. "You're a lost cause." She took a step towards the doorway. "I'm going to get changed."

Amos stepped out of the Void. "Wear these." He shoved a bundle of black leather at her before disappearing again.

"Where would he have got these from?" She

struggled to hold onto the leather garments and not let the blanket slip.

Roy shrugged. "You're probably better off not asking."

She started to, then changed her mind and headed for her room where she changed into the clothes. The leather trousers were a little big on her, sitting low on her hips, while the vest was slightly tight. The clothes felt odd. Nothing like what she normally wore. Taking a deep breath, she returned to the lounge room. "I'm going to need a set of these that fit better."

"They're not that easy to come by."

"Leather?" Claire frowned. "You mean they're expensive."

"That too, but it's dragon leather."

Claire caught a glimpse of Nate's stunned expression and wouldn't have been surprised to learn she looked the same. "Dragons! Who killed them? Amos?"

"No, but he's killed more than his fair share. He is a Knight," Roy said.

She pointed a finger at him. "I told you that isn't the answer to every question."

Nate moved closer to Claire, holding out an arm to her. "Pinch me. I really hope I'm not asleep."

"That won't help." She punched him in the arm, smiling sweetly. "That's for laughing at me."

Nate rubbed his arm, grinning. "I laughed at Harold too."

"Want me to give you one from him?"

"Nah, it'd be a waste of time. That old man looks fragile. You'd have to break your hand and hardly hurt me for it to be from him."

"Are you two always like this? Weren't we talking about dragon leather a second ago?" Roy frowned. "We need to focus on what we're going to do about Wayne and his group."

"We were working on that," Claire said.

"You were joking about Harold."

Nate nodded once. "Exactly. Which is good. Now we know we can't turn to him for help. Unless we need cannon fodder. Or whatever the equivalent would be with Knights and dragons." He turned to Claire. "So unfair I don't get to be a dragon too. I'd make an awesome dragon."

Chapter Twelve

Claire stepped in front of Roy when he tried to leave the room. "Where are you going?"

"They will kill us." He held her gaze a moment. "This is serious. Stanley especially won't want to hand us over. Not now he knows you're a dragon. They killed his parents when he was five."

She pressed her hand against his chest, the beat of his heart steady beneath her palm. "I'm sorry. Nate and I are terrible together. The bigger the fight we're going into, the more we joke around. I know Wayne is serious. And the rest of them. I was there when they pointed guns at us."

"Guns? Do I get a gun since I don't get to be a dragon?" Nate asked.

"Can you use a gun?" Roy moved so he could see Nate, but not enough that he dislodged Claire's hand.

"Yep."

"Really?" Roy sounded sceptical.

"His first dad liked to go hunting and taught him how to use guns," Claire said.

"Second Dad," Nate corrected.

"The biological one doesn't count. He wasn't there long enough to be a dad."

Nate shrugged. "He was still my dad." He looked to Roy. "Do I get a gun?"

"Not unless things get desperate," Roy muttered.

"I've got a feeling things probably already are, but you don't want to admit it." Claire took another step closer to him, her hand remaining on his chest, almost no space between them.

"I know what desperate looks like, and this isn't it."

"What does it look like?" She held his gaze, for a second wishing Nate wasn't in the room.

"Blood and dead bodies."

There was a haunted quality to his tone and a look in his eyes that made her believe he'd seen desperate. "Then in that case, I wouldn't want to miss the chance to do this."

"Do w-"

Her lips met Roy's, cutting off his words. Her hand slid up his chest and behind his neck when he returned her kiss.

"All right. That's enough," Nate muttered.

Claire pulled back to meet Roy's gaze, grinning. "I don't know about that. What do you think?"

Roy grinned fleetingly, taking her hand from around his neck and threading his fingers through hers. "That we've got a lot to do. Stanley and Wayne are Knight Mages. Stronger than your typical human, not really mages at all except for their ability to use caged Pliethins to travel through the Void and see Hell Hounds when they wear the skin of other people and creatures."

Claire looked down at herself. "Like I'm wearing the skin of a dragon?"

"No. Nothing like that. Like they are the other person or creature."

"How can this entire world exist without every single person on Earth noticing it?" Nate asked.

"Those who do notice try to find their place or risk death."

"I really wish you hadn't said that," Claire muttered.

Roy's hand tightened on hers. "I'll teach you to protect yourself." He turned so he could see Nate. "Both of you."

"Then do I get a gun?" Nate asked.

"A sword is often better against a dragon." Roy said.

"Where's your sword?" Nate's gaze went to Roy's hip. "It's not like you can wander around wearing a weapon."

Roy drew a dagger out of the side of his boot. "That's why I tend to carry a couple of these."

"Nice. A couple of those would be all right. But a gun is always good. You can take your opponent out from a distance," Nate said.

"Dragons are faster than you think." Roy was in front of Nate, the dagger held at his throat before either of them could move.

"Let him go." Claire's voice was hard.

Roy sheathed his dagger. "I wouldn't hurt him. I wanted you both to understand what you'll face."

"I'm a dragon. I'll be able to move that fast." Claire raised her chin. "If a dragon comes for me I'll turn into a dragon and fight it."

"Can you fly?"

She shrugged.

"Do you know how to protect your wings so they aren't torn to shreds?"

Nate spoke before Claire, who'd opened her mouth, could. "Then maybe you better start teaching us instead of telling us everything we can't do."

"I'm ready whenever you are," Roy said.

"I'm not. I've got to do homework and we need

to get started on the spare bedroom if you're having your friend visit you here, Nate," Claire said.

"No." Roy looked from one to the other. "Yes to homework since you need to make certain no one realises what's going on, but no wasting time unpacking boxes and no inviting people over who might end up being caught in the line of fire."

Nate swore. "Guess there goes that potential relationship." He grinned. "Although I guess dragons are better than some girl."

Claire crossed her arms over her chest and gave Nate a narrow eyed look. "You better not be dumping all girls together in that comment."

"Nah. All but you." With a grin, Nate ducked behind Roy, who sighed loudly.

Claire still managed to punch Nate in the arm, grinning now he wasn't.

"This is going to take weeks," Roy muttered.

Claire snagged his hand, meeting his gaze, a slight smile in place. "We might surprise you. It's one of the things we're serious about." She paused a moment. "Want to help us with our homework so we get it done quicker?"

* * *

The next morning, Claire staggered around the

house, sending daggered looks at Roy, who she had renamed the sadistic slave driver. "Why don't you look as bad as we do?" She eyed him up and down. "We took you down a couple of times." She avoided mentioning they'd cheated and been not the slightest bit honourable in their methods.

"I'm a Knight."

Nate glared at Roy, a spoonful of cereal halfway to his mouth. "I see what you mean. I reckon we should beat the crap out of him every time he says that."

"Do you think you're capable of doing that?" Roy asked.

"We took you down last night," Claire pointed out.

"Only by subterfuge. Kissing Wayne or Stanley won't help."

"What about Tobiah?" Claire asked.

Roy shrugged. "I don't know him, but since he's a Knight Mage, more than likely not."

"Would it help if I was the one to kiss them?" Nate pushed his empty bowl away, leaning back in his chair to stretch.

"They'd probably prefer that to a dragon." Roy rose from the table collecting his and Nate's empty bowl.

Claire finished her last mouthful and held the bowl

out. She smiled when he took it. "Thanks." She turned to Nate. "You staying here again tonight?"

He nodded. "If you don't mind. By the time the sadistic slave driver is finished with us I'm incapable of moving."

"I better check on Bub before I finish getting ready for school." He was in the laundry, where he'd retreated after one of them had stood on him. She stopped in the kitchen doorway to look back at Nate and Roy. "Poor dog. Clipped, trampled and laughed at." She pointed at Nate when she said the last two words.

Nate grinned unrepentantly. "I checked online before I fell asleep last night. His hair won't be full length before your mum is back. You are dead. No need to worry about Knights, fanatical Knight Mages or dragons. Your mum is going to kill you."

Claire groaned. "Maybe I'll get lucky and they'll be having such a great honeymoon they'll extend it."

"I still say get it over and done with now. Give her time to get it out of her system before she sees you," Nate said.

"Like that has helped before," Claire muttered as she headed to the laundry. She tried not to smile when she was greeted by Bub's mournful expression. "The new hairstyle isn't my fault and what did you think you were doing jumping around us when we were training last night?" His expression remained mournful. "No point looking at me like that." She paused a moment. "Do you need to go outside again?" Roy had let Bubbles out earlier and the annoying dog had come the moment Roy had called. "Well, traitor?"

The dog turned his head away, looking towards the wall.

"Be like that," she muttered, turning away to run into Roy. "Sorry."

"Are you okay? I didn't work you too hard last night?"

"I feel a little sore, but not too bad. Probably not as bad as Nate." She paused, expecting him to speak. "Is something wrong?"

"Why did you kiss me last night?"

"You've waited until now to ask me?"

"It's the first moment we've been alone." Roy waited a moment, eventually speaking again. "Why?"

"Because I wanted to. Is there any other reason to kiss someone? Why? Were you hoping I wouldn't kiss you again?"

"You haven't."

"Did you expect me to make all the moves?"

"Does that mean you're interested in kissing me again?"

Grinning, Claire closed the distance between them. "Haven't you learned that I tend to say exactly what I mean?"

"I wasn't sure that would extend to everything."

"Yeah, it does." She slid her arms around his neck. "Your move."

A grin fleetingly appeared before Roy lowered his head, his lips brushing lightly across hers. He raised his head enough to be able to meet her gaze. "I'll always be in the precarious position of being both a Knight and a dragon."

"I tend to join fights that are impossible to win because I'm not going to give in to bullies. Life isn't fair, but that doesn't mean we should let it be that way."

"If you were trying to offer a negative to make me feel better about mine, you actually offered me a positive."

"How is that a positive?"

Roy grinned.

She rolled her eyes. "Don't tell me. Let me guess. You're a Knight."

"Exactly." His lips met hers again and they remained wrapped in each other's arms until Nate called out to them to hurry up or he and Claire would be late to school.

Claire drew away from Roy, her hands remaining around his neck, her arms stretched as far as possible. "What are you doing today?"

"Amos wants me to learn more about my dragon side since I've held a Pliethin. He said there are some abilities we'll find useful. Like being able to travel through the Void eventually."

"Will I be able to do that?"

"I don't know. You're not the typical dragon. Who knows what you'll be capable of."

She grinned. "Big things. I've always been destined for big things."

Nate stepped into the laundry. "Yeah, like big amounts of detention. You did say we'd go in the same car. Hurry up or I'll leave without you."

"We're going in my car today, yours tomorrow."

"You expect me to sit passenger?"

She started to move away from Roy, changing her mind at the last second to lean forward and give him one more kiss before turning to Nate and holding her hand out for the keys. "Yes, and you're going to love every minute of it."

"Yeah, right. We've already decided this isn't a nightmare."

"Don't you mean dream?" Keeping her hand out, she grabbed the keys from him with her other hand, holding them behind her back when it looked like he might try and take them, her other hand raised to fend him off.

"No, I said exactly what I meant. Nightmare." He strode away, glancing over his shoulder. "Come on." Another glance over his shoulder. "See you, Roy."

Chapter Thirteen

Claire started to follow Nate, changing her mind and turning back for one last kiss. Grinning, she hurried after Nate, grabbing her schoolbag on the way outside, tugging her cap down low. She couldn't help glancing in the direction where Roy had told her the Knights were hiding. It was an effort not to keep looking, but she didn't want to give away that they knew Knights were hidden there.

They both remained silent until they were a couple of streets away from school. Nate placed his hand on Claire's shoulder. "Thanks for including me in all this. Would you have told me if you hadn't accidentally changed?"

"I'd planned to convince Roy after I showed him the picture."

Nate chuckled. "Dragon Lady. No wonder you

were amused." He sobered. "What are you going to do if you change during a fight?"

"I nearly did against Linden, but your voice grounded me."

"Plenty of back answering and smart arse comments then. I can manage that easily."

It was Claire's turn to chuckle. "We both can. It's what gets us in the most amount of trouble."

They remained silent again for a bit, Nate the one to break the silence again. "Do you think they have a plan?"

"No."

"If the fanatical guys have people to call for help, why doesn't Amos? Aren't we meant to be on the good guys' side?"

"I'm not sure if there is a good and bad side."

"Yeah, there is. The bad guys are always fanatics so that makes us the good guys by default."

Another smile escaped. "Somehow I don't think any of our teachers would agree with that logic. Speaking of teachers makes me think of school and lunchtime. What's happening today?"

By the time Nate had finished telling her which student was being picked on and which one was going after him, and they'd discussed some possible plans, they pulled up in front of the school as the bell rang. They had to run or risk getting detention for being late.

The day seemed to pass slowly and Claire found herself drifting off a few times during class. Roy had worn her out more than she'd thought. Which wasn't good since they had a fight to face during lunch. The bully wasn't expecting them, only his victim. She tried not to smile at that thought. Her teacher would want to know what she found so amusing if she did.

When the bell rang for lunch, Claire ate on the way to the location, Nate joining her before she was halfway there, draping an arm around her shoulders. They arrived in time to see their classmate being pushed up against a tree, protesting that it wasn't his fault the homework wasn't finished. Sometimes the unexpected occurred.

The other boy's hand curled into a fist. "Like a broken nose?"

Claire stepped away from Nate. "I don't know. Why don't you come over here and we'll find out?"

"This has got nothing to do with you." The boy glared at each of them equally.

Nate stopped an arm's length away from Claire. "That's where you're wrong. We've decided we want to make it our business. So what are you going to do about it?"

The boy nodded towards the crowd forming and two boys joined him.

"Is that all you got?" Nate sounded both disappointed and surprised.

"That was my thought too." Claire grinned. "Almost like you read my mind."

Another boy stepped out of the crowd. He was the largest of them all. "How about four against two?"

Claire shared a look with Nate. "Now that's better, but how are we going to decide who fights which one? I guess we could draw straws."

"I have no straws. We could roll dice. Throw an odd number and you get the stupid ones."

Claire's hands went to her hips, her grin firmly in place. "How can you tell the difference?"

One of them roared, rushing towards her.

"Guess you figured it out." Nate threw himself at one of the other boys, his fists loud as they slammed into him.

Claire sidestepped, sticking out a foot to trip the one who'd overshot her. "Is it me or does this seem easier compared to the sadistic slave driver?" Her fist hit one of them in the stomach and he doubled over, gasping for breath. She spun to see the second one was backing away, ignoring his mate who demanded he help. "That was it? How lame is this getting?"

Nate's second opponent did the same as hers, backing away as his first opponent crashed face first into the dirt.

Nate crouched beside the boy sprawled in the dirt, people continuing to come closer to see what was going on. "What was that you said about the unexpected occurring?"

The boy struggled to get to his feet, not answering.

Claire joined Nate, her opponent doing the smart thing and staying down. "You will leave that kid alone." She gestured towards their classmate. "Or we'll break your nose."

"One day you'll get what you deserve," the boy snarled.

Claire laughed. "I already have and I'm loving every minute of it." She glanced at Nate. "How about you?"

"I think you got the better part of the bargain, but other than that I can't complain."

The boy took a step away from them. "You're crazy."

"Absolutely." She slung an arm around Nate's shoulders.

"Strange. You wouldn't think he'd be complimenting us after I punched him," Nate said.

The boy continued to back away, shaking his head.

"One day you're going to get killed taking on more than you can handle."

Nate slowly nodded. "He could be right."

Claire grinned. "Probably."

The boy gave them one last look, a wary one that had more than a touch of fear in it, before turning and hurrying away.

Claire glanced around, seeing that all of them had gone, even the one she'd left in the dirt. "That was rather lame. Nothing like facing the sadistic slave driver."

"Nope. Not at all. I think we're going to have to find bigger challenges."

Before Claire could comment, their classmate came over to them. "Thank you. Did you want me to do your homework for you?"

Claire stared at him, stunned by his offer. "No. Why would you ask that?"

"Don't you want me to pay for your protection?"

She sighed. "Go away before you annoy me."

Their classmate scurried away, the crowd having already dispersed.

"Why does everyone expect the worst?" She stared after the boy.

"Because that's typically what they get." Nate glanced around the area. "I was looking forward to that fight. Thought it'd last longer than that. How about you figure out how to use that super powered hearing of yours. You might be able to hear someone calling for help."

"And then what? We slip into a phone booth and change into our capes and masks?" she asked dryly.

Nate chuckled. "Sounds good to me."

"Unless you want me to turn into something else, my hearing isn't about to improve." She thought of when she'd held the fire in her hands. "Actually…" She raised her hand and stared down at her palm, trying to make the fire form.

"What are you doing?"

She frowned at Nate before returning her attention to her palm. How had Amos made it form? She thought of the sensation, a flicker of red appearing for a split second, sounds and smells rushing in on her to fade along with the flame.

"Now that was cool. Do it again."

She glared at Nate. "If you'd shut up, I might actually have a chance to figure out how to do it." She was still trying to make fire form in the palm of her hand when the bell rang. Lowering her hand she sighed heavily. "What good is any of this if I can't use it?"

"You'll figure it out."

"I guess. But it's taking too long."

Nate grinned. "You've always been impatient." He draped an arm around her shoulders. "Let's get to class before we're late and end up with detention. I don't know about you, but I've got better things to do than sit around school all afternoon." He walked towards class, keeping Claire at his side. "We need to figure out how to beat the sadistic slave driver without resorting to distractions. There's only one of him."

"There might be. But don't forget, he's a Knight." She grinned at Nate's groan.

"I'll beat the crap out of you too if you start using that as an answer."

Still grinning, she slipped out from under his arm, heading to her own classroom, glancing over her shoulder. When he grinned back at her, she waved.

The rest of the school day seemed to pass ridiculously slow and Claire found herself trying to bring flames to her palm, her hand in her lap and hidden from view by her desk. Several times she managed a flicker of red before it vanished, taking with it scents and sounds.

Reaching home that afternoon, Claire spoke to Roy before the front door was closed. "I want to learn how to use fire."

"You'd need a Dragon Mage to teach you about that and I'm not about to involve them until Wayne and Stanley are no longer after Amber."

She stopped in front of Roy, dropping her schoolbag on the floor, reaching for him as Nate left the room headed in the direction of the kitchen. "Surely you know other Dragon Mages."

"I'll ask Uncle Amos if he can help-" He broke off, pulling away from her. "Nate can see people in your backyard. I heard him muttering about them."

She followed him to the kitchen, staring out the window, wishing her hearing was as good as Roy's. All the time, not only when she changed form or created fire. "Where are they?"

"In the shrubs by the broken palings." Nate pointed.

Seeing Stanley and a girl around her age peering into Roy's backyard, she started to stride to the kitchen doorway.

Roy grabbed hold of her, pulling her against him. "You're not going out there."

"They're in my backyard." She glared at him, unable to escape. "Let me go."

"Who are they?" Nate asked.

She continued to meet Roy's gaze. "Let. Me. Go."

"They don't know you're here. They don't know any of us are here." Roy continued to hold her.

"They don't know who I am. What if I go out and ask them what they're doing?" Nate asked.

Claire turned in Roy's arms to stare at Nate. "No fighting without me."

"Don't risk it," Roy said. "That's Jennifer, Wayne's daughter. She's worse than her father."

"I don't care who they are. They're not welcome in Claire's backyard." Nate strode from the room, taking out his phone.

Roy moved to the window, continuing to hold Claire.

"You can let me go. I'm not about to go after Nate unless they try and hurt him." She peered out the window.

Jennifer turned to face Nate, a fake smile in place, her sandy blond hair cut extremely short. "I'm looking for my dog. A small, brown one about this big." She held up her hands to indicate the size.

"I don't care if it's a designer dog worth a couple of thousand. Get out of my backyard. Next time try knocking on the front door and asking before wandering onto someone's property."

Jennifer took a step towards him, Stanley remaining at the broken palings, peering through to

Roy's yard. "Well now I'm here…" Her voice trailed off, her smile remaining in place.

Nate held up his phone. "I'll call the cops if the two of you don't go."

"Are you home alone?" Jennifer came closer to him.

Chapter Fourteen

Claire was almost relieved that Roy kept hold of her arm when she saw Jennifer's expression. She wanted to run out there and tell her to back off. The only time she'd seen an expression like that was on the face of a predator when watching a movie. Right before it attacked its prey.

"Not that it's any of your business, but no, I'm not," Nate said. "You've got till the count of three to get out of here before I ring the cops."

Stanley faced them. "He's not here. We'll look somewhere else." He strode towards the front of the house without waiting for Jennifer.

She smiled up at Nate, her expression not changing. "It was lovely meeting you." She drew out the word 'lovely'.

"Not in the slightest." Nate held her gaze, his arms remaining at his sides. "Now out."

Jennifer reached for him, her smile not faltering, her hand open.

Nate blocked her before she could touch his face. "Now." His tone was harsh.

Claire tried to pull away from Roy. His grip tightened. "Let me go." She kept her voice low, not knowing if Jennifer could hear as good as Roy.

Jennifer laughed, continuing to meet Nate's gaze. "You have no idea." She spun on her heel and strode off in the direction Stanley had taken.

When Nate followed Jennifer, Claire tried to go after him. "Roy." She filled his name with a warning.

"Do you want to get him killed?"

She stopped trying to pull away from him. "No. But what if they attack him?"

"There's no reason they should. They have no idea what he knows."

"If anything happens to him..." She let her warning trail off.

"I'm listening to what is happening. We can be out there before anything goes wrong."

"Then what is happening?"

"Nate stopped at the corner of the house. Stanley and Jennifer kept walking past my hearing range. He's coming back now."

The moment Roy let go of her, she ran to the back

door, grabbing hold of Nate and dragging him inside. "What were you thinking? You followed them!"

"They went into Harold's yard."

"What for?" Letting go of Nate, she turned to Roy who had joined them in the laundry. "Should we check on him?"

"I rang Uncle Amos. He said he'd be here shortly and not to do anything stupid."

Amos stepped out of the Void. "I said not to do anything else stupid."

Nate grinned. "You were probably wasting your breath saying something like that."

Amos stepped up to Nate. "Was I?"

Claire turned on Roy when he dragged her back from Amos. "Let me go."

Roy continued to hold her.

Nate stepped around Amos, grabbing Roy's arm. "You heard her. Let her go."

Amos threw up his hands. "I'm wasting my time here. This pair will get themselves killed worrying too much about the other and not enough about themselves."

Roy released Claire. "Just like a Knight."

Claire went to Nate, grabbing hold of his hand to stand protectively beside him.

Amos pointed a finger at Roy. "No. Absolutely not."

Remaining next to Nate, Claire turned to get a better look at Roy and Amos. "What is going on?"

Amos faced her. "You don't listen well enough to be a Knight. Neither of you do."

Nate shrugged. "Fine by me. I'd rather be a Dragon Mage." He grinned. "If I can't be a dragon that seems like the next best thing."

"Who says he can't be a dragon?" Claire turned to Roy. "We could do everything the same as what you and I did."

"Except for the mouse part. I want to be able to turn into something better than a mouse," Nate said.

"No." Amos crossed his arms over his chest. "We are not making dragons."

Roy looked from Claire to Nate. "It might be worth figuring out."

"Why?" Amos demanded.

Roy faced his uncle. "Then we could claim that we've always been Knights. That we have no dragon ancestors. Don't you get sick of hiding who you are?"

Amos remained silent a moment. "That might work. I'll talk to Isaac about it. Don't go doing anything until I have a chance to discuss it with him." He turned to Claire. "In the meantime, you need to learn how to change form properly. Get dressed into your dragon leathers."

She wanted to tell him not to order her around, but she did need to learn. She also wanted to ask him to teach her how to summon fire. Or find someone who could teach her. "I'll only be a minute." She grabbed her schoolbag from the lounge room before she went to her bedroom, leaving it on the floor near her door before closing it and getting changed. She started to pick up her phone from where she'd placed it on her dressing table while changing her clothes. Her trousers and vest had no pockets. And what was she meant to do with it when she changed form?

After a few seconds, she grabbed it, deciding to ask Amos. He obviously carried a phone and she hadn't seen him set it aside when he'd turned into a dragon. She found them in the kitchen, Amos and Nate arguing. "What do I do with my phone?"

"Leave it behind." Amos kept his gaze on Nate.

"You keep yours on you." His words sank in. "What? We're going somewhere? I didn't agree to that."

Amos stepped past Nate, grabbed Claire's phone and threw it to Roy, who caught it, and took hold of her hand.

The world reformed before she had time to protest

or pull away. "Where are we?" She looked around, stepping away from him when he let go of her hand. They were in an industrial building. Most of it was open, a partitioned off section to one side.

"Same place you stayed on the weekend."

"I want my phone." She wasn't about to let him think he could order her around. Or take her places without asking first.

"Do you want to learn or do I let Stanley have you?"

She smiled. He didn't know that she wouldn't let anyone risk themselves for her. "Would you let Stanley have Roy?" Her smile vanished when Amos came at her.

His fingers dug into her shoulder. "You will not get him killed or you will also die."

"Then don't threaten me. Roy promised to look after me. He gave me his oath. So teach me how to be a dragon so he doesn't have to get himself killed trying to protect me. And show me again how to call flames to my hands."

He held her gaze a moment before he stepped back with a nod. "You will learn and you will get out of Roy's life the moment you don't need him to look after you."

Her chin rose automatically, her hands becoming

fists. "I'll learn and I'll protect myself. I never hide behind anyone. I always fight my own battles."

Amos met her gaze a moment longer. "I see why you interest him." He unbuttoned his shirt and tossed it to the side. "But you will get out of his life. He doesn't need your kind of trouble."

"He's eighteen. Old enough to decide what kind of trouble he wants in his life." She felt Amos in her mind a moment before he spoke.

"*Focus. You will learn how to change form as easily as you breathe. Then we will work on fireballs.*" He became a dragon, stalking towards her.

The menacing figure approaching caused her to automatically become a dragon, stepping forward to meet him.

"*Not thoughtlessly. Consciously. Now try again.*" He became human.

It took her longer to change forms this time. Becoming a dragon was easier when Amos was in front of her. His attitude brought the fighter out in her and the dragon part was the strongest. The couple of times he tried to get her to turn into a mouse were futile. She couldn't do it. Not with Amos looking like he wanted to attack.

They spent hours changing forms, spending less than an hour working on Claire creating fireballs. She was exhausted when he grabbed his shirt. It was only her determination not to show weakness to Amos that had kept her training.

"I have dinner plans. I can't waste all night on you." He pulled on his shirt, doing up the buttons.

"What's the time?"

"Almost nine."

No wonder she was hungry. "What time are you having dinner?"

"Nine." He grabbed hold of her arm. "Practice turning into a mouse. You need to learn both your forms."

Before she could tell him he hadn't left himself much time to get to wherever he was going, they were stepping out of the Void into her laundry and he was gone again. She leaned against the back door, too exhausted to move. It wasn't Stanley, Wayne or Tobiah who would kill her. It was Amos with his determination to train her.

Roy stopped in the doorway of the laundry. "Are you okay?"

"Have you ever been trained by your uncle?"

Roy chuckled. "There's food keeping warm in the oven for you. Nate did your homework. Said that you need to copy it down so it's in your handwriting. And go over the typed stuff to make sure it sounds like it was written by you rather than him."

"Where is he?" She finally managed to push herself away from the door. "And where is Bub. He's unusually quiet."

"Nate nearly fell asleep at the table during dinner." Roy grinned fleetingly. "Apparently I made him train too hard. He's in bed now."

"Must be a genetic thing," she muttered as she followed Roy to the kitchen. "And Bub?"

"My mum is looking after him. I was hoping it would distract her from going after Stanley like she wanted to. And he kept getting underfoot while we were training."

Claire collapsed on one of the kitchen chairs, leaning against the table as she yawned. "Is this how hard you train to be a Knight?"

"Harder. But we work up to it. The younger ones don't put in as many hours as the older ones." Roy placed a plate of food and some cutlery in front of her.

"When do you go to school?" She picked up the cutlery.

"That is at school. We also learn the usual things you learn, which is why we board at our school."

"Have you finished training?"

Roy shrugged. "You never finish learning, but I have finished at the school."

She frowned, something in his tone making her think it hadn't been a good finish. "Were you thrown out?"

"Not exactly. But I'm not all that welcome since I'm friends with too many dragons. I tend to go there rarely." A wry smile made a brief appearance. "So you can see why I'm trying to avoid letting them know I'm part dragon."

Looking down at her plate, she was surprised to find she'd eaten the food already. She supposed she had been starving. "I need to go to bed. I'll have to get up earlier than usual to do my homework in the morning." She staggered to her feet.

Roy was in front of her in seconds, his arms going around her. "Are you okay?"

She smiled, her arms going around him. "This is nice."

"That didn't answer my question."

"I'm okay. Beyond exhausted, but okay." She nearly squealed when he lifted her into his arms, striding towards her bedroom. "I can walk." She didn't protest too strongly, sliding her arms around his neck.

"It's okay to accept help. It doesn't make you weak."

"Would your Amber accept help like this?" One hand slid down to his chest, running over the hard planes beneath his shirt, feeling the movement of muscles under her palm.

"She isn't my Amber. There are too many dragons with claims on her for any Knight to have a claim."

"Does that bother you?"

He turned sideways to step into Claire's room. "No. I admire her. Like I would admire another warrior." He placed her on the bed.

She drew him back to her when he started to move away. "Have you ever thought about her in any other way?"

He sat on the edge of the bed, a smile forming. "We were enemies when we first met. The only thing I felt for her was resentment and fear. It didn't take me long to admire her. Not only for her talents as a warrior, but for her loyalty to her people. There was never a time I thought of her romantically. She's a friend. Like Nate is your friend."

"Nate is more than a friend. He's family. Like a brother." She kept her hands entwined at his neck, smiling up at him. "Are you going to kiss me goodnight?"

Roy chuckled softly. "Do you always say what you think?"

"Mostly. Is that a problem?"

"No. That's one of the things I like about you."

Before she could ask what other things he liked, his lips met hers and she forgot her question.

Chapter Fifteen

The rest of the week was spent training. Amos trained Roy while Nate and Claire were at school and collected Claire every second day. Roy trained her and Nate the rest of the days. Nate didn't get a break while she trained with Amos. Roy kept him busy learning how to fight. Claire finally managed to change into a dragon on command, but couldn't become a mouse no matter how hard she tried. It was like the creature was too far from who she was for her body to be comfortable changing into such a little creature. But she did learn how to create fireballs, tempted more than once to create them at school and throw them at the people who annoyed her. She made do with throwing punches, nearly getting caught by a teacher on Thursday. She had moved from the area quickly, her sense of hearing having picked up in time to get her out of there without a second to spare.

They continued to see Stanley in the area, occasionally there were others with him. He mostly remained across the road and a few times Claire suggested they check on Harold, but both Roy and Nate refused to let her. Nate wanted to improve his ability to fight first. Roy didn't want to go at all. He didn't believe the bitter old man was worth risking her life. She kept arguing that he was supposed to be a Knight. He argued that all they were honour bound to guard people from were dragons and Hell Hounds.

By Sunday lunch, Claire was sick of training and sick of spending every moment at home, school or an empty industrial building. She stepped to the side instead of blocking Roy. "I want to go somewhere."

"No." Roy attacked again.

She avoided him. "I haven't been anywhere in ages. That includes last weekend. Being stuck in a cell doesn't count."

Roy lowered his hands and stepped close. "It's too dangerous."

She moved closer so they were toe to toe. "So we hide in here forever? My dad will be home next weekend for a week. It's going to be a little difficult for all of us to stay here."

"When does he arrive?" Roy asked.

"Next Sunday and leaves the following Saturday. Don't go changing the subject. I'm going out today. With or without you."

"Why don't you ask your uncle to magic you somewhere and we can meet you there?" Nate asked.

Roy kept his gaze on Claire. "It isn't magic. It's travelling through the Void."

Nate shrugged. "For someone who only sees people disappear, it's magic."

"Uncle Amos would say the same. It's too dangerous."

This time it was Claire who shrugged. "So? Do you think I care what your uncle thinks? I want to go flying. And I can't do it around here."

"Are you crazy?" Roy demanded.

She answered him with a smile.

"Can you give me a ride?" Nate asked. "Since I can't fly."

Roy finally looked away from Claire long enough to give Nate the same exasperated look. "How have the two of you managed to live as long as you have?"

Nate grinned. "Magic?"

Claire returned Nate's grin. "Sounds about right to me."

"Why would you want to take the risk?" Roy asked.

"Because I'm not about to sit in a prison watching life pass me by. Are you?"

"Aren't I here too?" Roy asked.

"Why are you here?" She had a feeling he'd normally be one of the ones out there fighting.

"Training you and Nate."

"What would you be doing if you weren't training us?" Claire persisted.

"Bet he'd be tracking down the fanatics," Nate said.

Roy reached for her hands. "Claire..."

She stepped back, avoiding him. "I don't have a fancy name."

Roy's lips slowly curved into a smile as he reached for her again. "Okay. But wait until dark."

She stepped into his embrace. "Where will we go? We have school tomorrow."

"Somewhere deserted. A couple of hours from here. We don't want to be spotted by anyone."

"I'm going too," Nate said.

Claire looked around Roy's shoulder. "Of course you are." She grinned when she heard Roy's sigh, turning her gaze on him. "You weren't thinking of leaving my best friend behind. It's not like we were planning some romantic outing."

"Are you sure it wouldn't be a romantic outing?"

Her breath caught in her throat at his expression. "Is it?"

Roy held her gaze a moment longer before smiling. "Maybe next time. Nate probably deserves a break too after the progress he's shown this week."

"Yes!" Nate victory punched the air. "I'm going flying."

"Can you ride a horse?" Roy asked Nate.

"Yeah."

Roy nodded. "You can go flying."

Claire met Nate's gaze, returning his grin.

The rest of the afternoon passed slowly and Claire found it as difficult to concentrate as Nate seemed to. Several times Roy warned them that they needed to learn to concentrate no matter what else was going on. Claire was glad when it was finally dark enough that they could leave, rolling her eyes when Roy insisted they wear hoodies, the hoods drawn up to shadow their faces.

When they were in her car, Nate in the back seat after numerous complaints, she headed in the direction Roy had given her. "I really don't think they would have had night vision goggles. Who has anything like that other than armies?"

"What do you think Knights are?" Roy asked.

The question stunned her. "They're an army?"

"What would you call a large armed group of people?"

Roy's question left her speechless. She hadn't thought about it like that. "Should we go home?" A handful of armed people hadn't seemed like that big a deal. How large a group were the Knights?

"No. That'd look suspicious," Roy said.

"Why didn't you tell us it was an army?" Nate asked.

"I thought you realised." Roy gestured towards the right. "Turn at the next street."

They remained silent, only Roy's directions interrupting the silence. Roy eventually directed Claire to pull up at a roadside stop. The area was deserted and looked like it was rarely used.

"Why here?" She turned off the engine, the headlights going out and plunging the area into darkness.

"No one lives around here and very few travel this road." Roy opened the car door, the interior light cutting through the darkness. "Leave your ordinary clothes behind."

"What about my car keys and phone?" Claire slipped the hoodie over her head.

"I've got pockets in my trousers." Roy tossed his hoodie onto the back seat next to Nate.

"How does that work?" Nate asked. "When you're a dragon what happens to the phone and keys?"

Roy shrugged as he got out of the car. "I have no idea and don't really want to know. It works. That's all I need to know."

Claire shuddered. "I think that's all I need to know too." She got out of the car, Nate getting out at the same time. "How will Nate be able to ride one of us? It's not like we have a saddle. And we're bigger than your average horse."

"The principal is the same." Roy turned to Nate. "Where did you put that rope I gave you earlier?"

"In the boot." Nate took the keys from Claire and opened the boot of the car, tossing the rope to Roy before returning the keys to Claire.

She slid her phone and keys into the side of her trousers. The items remained in place, the bulk of them enough to take up the slack in the waist. "I really need clothes that fit me better."

"Sorry," Roy said.

"It's not your fault." Claire glanced around the area before locking the car. "Do we change here or go somewhere else?"

Roy drew out one of his daggers, striding towards Nate. "You need to be able to hear us talk mentally."

Nate eyed the dagger. "This is gonna hurt, isn't it?"

"A bit." Roy took hold of Nate's hand and made a small cut.

Nate grinned. "That wasn't so bad."

"That was the easy part." Roy made a similar cut in his own hand.

"What next? Blood brothers?" Nate continued to grin.

"Not exactly." Roy slid the dagger back into his boot then pressed their cuts together.

Nate hissed, drawing his hand back the moment Roy let go. "What's in your blood? Acid?"

"Dragon blood."

Nate shook his hand. "How's that going to help me hear you?"

Claire mentally reached for Nate. *"Did it work?"*

Nate looked startled. "Yeah, it did." He grinned. "That is really cool. How long will it last?"

"Two to four weeks. Usually around two weeks." Roy made a slipknot in the rope so that it became an adjustable circle. "Put this over my head so you have something to hold onto while we're flying."

Nate took the rope Roy held out, his grin firmly in place. "Let's go."

Claire changed form a second before Roy, launching into the sky, the wind rushing at her face, the scents and sounds of the night surrounding her. Within minutes Roy was beside her, Nate on his back, giving a victory yell. Excitement rushed through her and she roared, her wings pumping up and down to shoot her forward.

Roy came alongside her. "*What do you think?*"

"*I was born to be a dragon.*" Spotting a rabbit, Claire dived towards the ground, pulling up at the last minute. A rumble rose out of her and this time she knew it was laughter. How could Roy not want to be a dragon? Didn't he realise how amazing it was? Before she could ask him, a creature came out of the night towards her.

"*Wyvern!*" Roy raced ahead, attacking the creature, going for its wings. "*Hold on, Nate.*"

"Why is it going for us?" Nate demanded.

His words were torn away by the wind, but Claire could hear them clearly enough. "*You said to stay out of deserted areas. Why bring us to one?*" She had no idea how to attack in dragon form. At least not while she was in the air.

Roy banked to the right, avoiding the claws of the wyvern. "*I didn't think one would attack when there are two of us. There must be more in the area.*"

"Careful. Are you trying to throw me off?" Nate asked.

"I'll land and you can get off. It'll be safer. Claire, distract the wyvern."

Chapter Sixteen

Claire wanted to protest. How did you distract something that wanted to tear you to shreds? When the wyvern went for Roy as he dived towards the ground, she attacked, her claws raking across its back.

The creature turned on her and she arrowed away, trying to avoid the sharp teeth that looked like they'd do as much damage as the claws. *What's taking you so long, Roy?* She slashed at the wyvern, her claws barely managing to harm it.

I'm giving Nate my phone so he can ring Amos and tell him we're at the place where he's been training me.

The wyvern managed to rake its claws along her side and she spun away, trying to keep her wings out of its way. The last thing she wanted to do was plummet to the ground. She doubted she'd survive that fall. *Well hurry up.*

"*I can smell your blood. Are you hurt badly?*" Roy demanded.

"*How do you know it's Claire's blood?*" Nate asked.

"*It smells like hers.*" Roy joined Claire, attacking the wyvern.

"*About time.*"

"*I'll distract it and you come at it from above. There are more on the way.*" Roy flew beneath the wyvern, circling around to come at it from the front again.

"*How can you tell?*" Claire flew away from the wyvern angling upwards before diving towards it.

"*You should be able to sense them too.*" Roy attacked the wyvern, his claws swiping the head of the creature before he angled away.

Claire waited until Roy attacked again before she dived on the wyvern, sinking claws into wings, shredding the thin membranes between the wing veins. The creature screeched, twisting in the air to try and reach her. Claire spun with it, clinging to its clawed wings. Every single part of the creature looked like it was built to attack.

"*Let go of it and drop away,*" Roy ordered.

A dragon came out of the Void. "*What do you lot think you're doing?*" Amos demanded.

Claire let go of the wyvern, plummeting towards the ground. It took her a moment to coordinate her wings and for a second she thought she might crash into the ground. She angled upwards, her heart racing as fast as she did.

The wyvern screeched again, spinning towards the ground, passing Claire midair.

She turned to watch it, wincing when it hit the ground with a thud. She looked away. "*Are we planning to leave it there?*"

"*The lot of you go home. What were you thinking coming out here like this?*" Amos swooped on the dead body, disappearing with the wyvern.

Roy headed to the ground. "*I'll get Nate, you go back to the car before the rest of the wyverns arrive.*"

She didn't obey, remaining above them in case the wyverns arrived before they could escape. She flew at Roy's side once he was in the air again, Nate on his back. "*Are you both okay?*"

"That was amazing," Nate said aloud. "When can we do it again?"

A rumble rose out of Claire. "*Actually, it wasn't too bad.*" Her wound was barely a scratch. She'd had far worse injuries from some of her fights against humans.

"*I should have known.*" Roy swooped towards the car, landing next to it.

Claire landed beside him, becoming human,

speaking aloud. "I need to learn how to fight as a dragon. I felt useless."

Amos stepped out of the Void. "The lot of you were useless."

"I want to try and become a dragon," Nate said.

Amos took a step towards him. "No. I've decided it's too dangerous."

Claire automatically stepped between them. "Yes."

Amos reached for Claire to push her out of the way. Nate grabbed his wrist.

Meeting Nate's gaze, Amos stepped even closer, letting Nate continue to hold his wrist. "You think you can take me on?"

"No, but that won't stop me from fighting at Claire's side."

"I thought she wasn't your girlfriend."

"She isn't. She's family." Nate continued to meet Amos' gaze.

Amos pulled his wrist from Nate's grip, pushing him away. "I want nothing to do with your experiments, but I won't stop you if you want to risk yourselves." He pointed a finger at Nate. "But you bring harm to Roy and you'll have our family to answer to."

"I'd never hurt a mate," Nate said.

Claire moved closer to Nate. "Neither of us would."

"Leave them alone, Uncle Amos. They're not our enemy."

Amos didn't move. "But are they our friends?"

Roy didn't hesitate. "Yes."

"Go home." Amos stepped back, vanishing into the Void.

No one spoke for a moment, Nate breaking the silence. "Does that mean I get to be a dragon?"

Claire grinned. "Sounds like it to me."

"Nothing was decided," Roy said.

Claire faced Roy. "We can't hide forever and you were the one who said we're only as strong as the weakest one on the team."

"As strong as the weakest one you stand beside."

"Yeah, that."

Roy hesitated. "Okay."

Claire grinned. "How do we get a caged Pliethin and dragon bone?"

"Any Knight can get dragon bone," Roy said.

"And the caged Pliethin?" Claire asked.

"Only Knight Mages have them. And a handful of Dragon Mages."

Claire met Nate's gaze, surprised she could see so clearly in the limited light. Then she realised she could still smell and hear better than normal. "Guess we need to find out where Stanley is."

Nate nodded. "Sounds good to me." He grinned. "Probably owe him for thinking he could wander into your yard without permission."

Claire returned his grin. "Amongst other things." She took the phone and keys out from where she'd tucked them in the waistband of her trousers, striding towards the driver's door. "I can sense wyverns above us. We should leave before they decide to do something about us killing one of them."

Roy got in the front seat. "Stanley isn't likely to be alone."

"That girl didn't look like she'd be much trouble." Nate closed the back door once he was in the car.

"She's a trained Knight, a year older than me and started training younger than I did," Roy said.

Claire patted Roy on the leg before starting the car. "Don't worry. We won't let her hurt you."

Roy chuckled. "I think it's the other way around."

"I'll turn into a dragon if I can't handle her as a human." Claire headed in the direction of home.

"Knights are trained to kill dragons. They know every vulnerability."

"Then we need to know how to kill dragons too," Claire said.

"Why?" Nate demanded.

Claire smiled. "So we know how to protect ourselves."

"We don't know that this will work." Roy turned in his seat to look at Nate. "You might not become a dragon. Anything could happen."

Nate shrugged. "I guess we'll soon see."

"What if it goes wrong?" Roy asked. "Have either of you thought of that?"

"We'll do everything the same as you did for me," Claire stated. She didn't want anything to happen to Nate, he was her best friend. Remaining human around her looked like it might be dangerous. The wyvern was a perfect example of that.

"There were a lot of things that could have contributed to you becoming a dragon. Including your genetics," Roy said.

"We need to get whatever the Knight Mages used to knock you two out. And we have to figure out everything else about the situation to give it the best chance of working." Nate took out his phone. "Was there anything special about the environment? I'll make notes, you two tell me every little detail no matter how insignificant."

The drive back to Claire's place consisted of discussions and arguments over what her and Roy remembered about being kidnapped. Nate made notes on everything from the concrete floor to the flannelette pyjamas Claire had been wearing, suggesting he wear clothes with cotton fibres in case that made a difference. By the time they arrived, Nate had a long list of everything they needed to recreate Claire's transformation.

Once they were in the lounge room, Nate pushed back his hood, grinning. "If this doesn't work then it was because Claire's a freak of nature."

"I am not a freak of nature." She glared at Nate.

Nate's grin remained in place. "Let's hope not. I want to be a dragon." He sidestepped when she half-heartedly tried to hit him.

"Stanley won't necessarily have a caged Pliethin with him," Roy said.

Claire frowned. "I don't recall him having one when he was in my yard." Her frown cleared, replaced by a smile. "We should return to the house they held us in. Maybe there are caged Pliethins there."

Roy slowly shook his head. "My uncle was right to be worried."

Claire shared a look with Nate. "I have no idea why everyone always thinks that."

Nate shrugged. "Got no clue either." His serious tone was ruined by a grin.

Claire grinned back at him before turning to Roy. "If you tell me where it is, we can go without you."

"No."

"What do you mean no?" Claire demanded. He better not try and stop them.

Roy came forward and took her hand. "I won't let you go back there alone."

She pulled out of his light grip and threw her arms around his neck. "Thank you." She pressed her lips against his.

"Must you?" Nate grumbled.

Claire drew back to smile at Roy, not bothering to glance at Nate. "Yes, I must." She kissed Roy again.

Chapter Seventeen

The week went by in a blur of school, training and trying to spy on Wayne and Stanley as they watched Roy's house. Friday afternoon, Claire, Roy and Nate sat in her kitchen eating sandwiches and trying to decide what to do next.

"Darrell is back Sunday." Nate took another bite of his sandwich.

"We have to do something before then." She couldn't wait another entire week before they tried to get a caged Pliethin and there was no way she wanted to go after one while her dad was at home.

"We can't rush these things," Roy said.

Nate's phone beeped and he checked the message, grinning. "Maybe we should rush these things. Mum wants to know if I've moved out of home and forgot to tell her."

Claire laughed. "Tell her you lost your way. Birds

ate the breadcrumbs." Her smile faded as she looked at Roy. "Tomorrow. We check out the house tomorrow. We have everything but the caged Pliethin."

Nate chuckled.

Claire turned to him. "What did she say?"

"That your dad will probably be annoyed to find that there aren't even crumbs left in the house. Get home and stop sponging off others."

Claire laughed. "Tell her you'll be home Sunday. We have plans."

"No we don't," Roy said.

She reached across the table and took Roy's hand, looking into his dark brown eyes. "Yes, we do."

He sighed. "What we have is nothing like a plan. It's a suicide mission."

She squeezed his hand. "Then we fly out of there before they can catch us and figure out something else."

Roy was silent a moment before he spoke. "We'll have an early night and drive over there a couple of hours before dawn. That'll give us a chance to watch the place for a bit. If it's occupied they're more than likely asleep. If it's deserted, we'll go in."

Claire grinned. "There you go. Now we have a plan."

"No, now we have a couple of ideas. No sensible Knight would go into a situation with so little information or idea of what to expect or what to do." Roy wrapped his other hand around their clasped hands. "This is more what you'd expect of a dragon."

Nate put his hand over the top of theirs. "Sounds good to me. Guess that means we're more like dragons than Knights."

Roy looked from Nate to Claire. "That's what I've always been afraid of." He drew his hands from theirs, rising from the table. "Training. Then dinner and bed."

Claire grinned, standing up. "Look at you making all these plans."

Nate followed them into the lounge room, chuckling. "He's a natural at it."

Claire laughed when Roy sent her a look to let her know he was unimpressed. She stepped forward, brushing her lips across his. "We've got this. Stop worrying." She stepped back. "Weren't you going to teach us how to take you down?"

Within minutes, laughter faded and they trained, the furniture having been left at the edges of the room. A few times Claire thought they were about to beat Roy, but each time he outsmarted them. But that didn't stop her from trying until it was time for dinner and bed.

She lay in her bed, staring at the ceiling, able to see better than usual in the dark. Her hearing was also working extremely well, as was her sense of smell. "Goodnight, Roy." She spoke softly, like he was next to her rather than on a mattress in the lounge room.

"Goodnight, Claire."

She smiled at the faint sound of his voice. "Stop worrying about tomorrow and go to sleep."

"You are the one keeping me awake."

She smiled at the humour she could hear in his voice. "I wanted to know if you could hear me. And if I could hear you."

"Running water makes it difficult to hear things."

"Okay. I'll keep that in mind." She rolled over, pulling the blankets up and snuggling under them. Not that she knew how that information would come in handy. They could speak in their minds if they needed to share secrets. She drifted off to sleep, going over the limited plan they had for the following day, woken by the alarm on her phone well before she was ready to get up.

Wincing, she struggled out of bed, trying to turn down her hearing as she turned off the alarm. "That was the worst way to wake up."

"What happened?" Roy asked sleepily.

For a second she thought he was in her room, then she realised his voice was coming from the lounge room. "Super loud alarm. I thought I'd turned my hearing down."

"You can reduce noise from areas, not necessarily all areas at once."

Clambering out of bed, she frowned. "How confusing."

Nate knocked on her door. "You up or did you turn your alarm off and go back to sleep?"

"As if I'd do that." She changed into her dragon leather clothes, trying to sound indignant.

"You want me to remind you of every time you've done that?" Nate remained outside her door.

She threw a pillow at her door. "Want me to rearrange your memories?"

Nate chuckled. "I'll start breakfast. Two eggs?"

"You're going to need to do better than that for an apology." She grabbed her phone and slid it into the waistband of her dragon leather trousers before opening the door.

"Bacon?"

"That's better." She walked with him to the kitchen where they found Roy cracking eggs.

Nate looked confused. "How did you know what

we wanted for breakfast?" He turned to Claire. "Did you tell him in his mind?"

"He heard us." Claire grinned. "Dragon powered hearing."

Breakfast was filled with joking between Claire and Nate while Roy remained mostly silent. Once the kitchen was cleaned, Claire wrapped her arms around Roy. "You worried? You were really quiet during breakfast."

"I don't want either of you to be hurt. But that wasn't why I was quiet. I was listening to you." He smiled. "You're noisier than my family. Unless my mother is angry and out for blood."

"Does that happen often?"

"A little too often." Roy leaned forward, his lips meeting hers for a moment. "You haven't changed your mind?"

"No."

Roy looked to Nate who was using his phone. "What about you?"

Nate grinned. "Hell no."

Claire drew away from Roy, catching hold of his hand. "Time to go. We need a caged Pliethin."

They wore hoodies, keeping the hoods pulled low to hide their faces, Claire muttering about armies and night vision goggles, Nate saying he wouldn't mind a pair. Claire waited until they were driving away from her house before she told him he wouldn't need them if he managed to turn into a dragon.

The drive was filled with questions, from Nate, about what it was like to be a dragon. Claire smiled and told him he'd find out soon enough. Roy kept telling them not to get their hopes up.

Claire pulled up across from the house they'd been held captive in, turning off the engine and looking at Roy who had reminded them once again not to get their hopes up. "There's nothing wrong with hoping. Nor trying to go after what you hope for."

Roy took hold of her hand. "No, but remember to balance that with the possibility that this mightn't work."

Nate peered out the back window. "How are we going to know if someone is in there?"

Claire grinned. "Hope they snore so we can hear them." She emphasised the word 'hope', surprised when Roy smiled.

"We'll go around to the back of the house. If we can't hear anything we'll find a way inside." Roy reached up to slide across the interior light switch so it wouldn't come on when they opened the doors.

Claire put her phone on silent before she got out of the car, slipping it and her keys into a pocket of her hoodie once she'd locked up. They slipped silently around the side of the house, pausing regularly to listen. Reaching the back door, they remained in the shadows by the house. Everything was silent.

"*Think the place is empty?*" Nate asked.

Claire grinned at hearing his voice in her head. "*Being able to speak like this is going to come in very handy. We won't get in trouble for talking in class anymore.*"

"*I can't hear anyone inside,*" Roy said.

Claire tried the door handle. It was locked. "*How are we going to get in?*"

"*I'll check the windows.*" Nate moved along the back of the house.

"*Sometimes they hide a key.*" Roy glanced around the area, checking under a rock and the two paving stones near the back door.

When his search only resulted in a spider scurrying away, Claire asked, "*What now?*"

"*I think I can get the bathroom window open, but I'm too large to go through it,*" Nate said.

Claire hurried to Nate's side. "*I could probably get through there. If someone helps me up.*"

Nate put the screen on the ground, leaning it against the house, then wriggled the pane of glass out of the frame and lowered it inside. *"Careful when you go in. The glass is sitting on the toilet. Don't knock it off. If we put it back in place they won't know how we got in."*

Claire grinned. That sounded good to her. Leave them wondering. Before she could ask who would help her, Roy wrapped his hands around her waist and lifted her towards the window. She put her arms through, turning sideways and struggling to pull herself through.

"A pity you can't turn into a mouse whenever you want," Nate said.

"It's not me. I'm nothing like a mouse so it makes it impossible to figure it out." She winced as she slid the rest of the way through the window and onto the toilet seat, trying not to let the windowpane fall.

"Not surprising that becoming a dragon suits you, Dragon Lady," Nate said.

She nearly laughed, a grin forming instead. *"Yep. Definitely dragon."* Setting the pane of glass on the floor, she awkwardly got to her feet, glancing around the bathroom. *"Give me a minute and I'll let the pair of you in through the back door."* She peered into a hallway. It was empty. The entire house had an empty feeling.

It wasn't until she entered the kitchen that she heard a sound. Like a chain scraping across a concrete floor. Her gaze was drawn down. They had someone in the cell? Anger rushed through her. She wasn't about to let them get away with keeping anyone locked up. Unlocking the back door, she stepped back to let Nate and Roy inside. "*I think there's someone in the cell downstairs.*"

"*I'll put the windowpane back in place in case we need to leave in a hurry.*" Nate strode out of the kitchen.

Roy grabbed Claire's arm before she could head downstairs. "*There's more than one person down there. Don't rush ahead without checking both sound and smell.*"

She tried to focus, but too many memories swamped her. Fear and anger fought with each other, a touch of revulsion at the thought of her claws slicing into Tobiah. Taking a deep breath, she crossed the kitchen to the door that led downstairs. The handle turned easily and she swung it open. The scent of Stanley came to her and she curled her hands into fists, forcing herself to remain where she stood, trying not to give into the anger that had her wanting to attack him.

"*Let's check what else is down here first. Stanley can wait. He's asleep.*" Roy rested a hand on her arm.

Claire nodded before stepping lightly down the stairs. She passed the closed doors along her left, stopping at the one on her right where they'd been held. The door handle turned easily, swinging open. The room was empty. She closed the door again and continued down the hallway, Roy at her side. The next door swung open as easily as the previous one, a bare bulb in the ceiling shining light on a girl chained and locked in the cell. There was a chair off to one side, nothing in the cell with the girl, and the smell of bleach hung in the room.

Chapter Eighteen

When the girl opened her mouth to speak, Claire raised a finger to her lips at the same time as Roy. "*We have to help her.*"

"*She's a dragon,*" Roy said.

"*I know. I can smell the scent on her.*" She tried to speak to her mentally. It was like there was no one there. "*Why can't I reach her mind? Even when you're blocking me I can tell you're there.*"

"*It's the chains they've used on her.*" Roy pressed his finger to his lips again when the girl opened her mouth.

She glared at them, moving her hands in a 'what can I do' motion. She wore a black dragon leather button up top and trousers that sat low on her hips, her hair a tangle of copper and gold around her face, her eyes dark enough they were almost black. Bruises, gashes and blood covered her body, very little of her golden coloured skin unmarked.

Nate joined them in the doorway. "*We can't leave her here.*"

"*We've got no way of setting her free. Those chains won't be easily broken. We'll need the key,*" Roy said.

"*Then we'll find the key.*" Surely it had to be somewhere nearby. She glanced around the room. There was nothing.

"*The moment we try and leave the room she'll call out,*" Roy warned.

"*I'll go over there and whisper our plan to her.*" Claire took a step forward.

Roy grabbed her arm and drew her back. "*She would be a fool to let you leave her side.*"

"*I'll go to her. Claire is right. We can't leave her here.*" Nate started to walk forward.

Roy grabbed hold of his arm too, meeting his gaze. "*Not all the dragons that Knights capture are innocent. Some are killers.*"

Nate pulled away from Roy. "*I'll take my chances.*" He smiled at Claire, when she momentarily rested her hand on his forearm, before striding to the cell.

The girl grabbed hold of him, pulling him against the bars. "Get me out of here."

Her voice was whisper soft, but Claire could clearly

hear the threat in her words. She started to run forward to help Nate, turning on Roy when his arms wrapped around her, keeping her from reaching her best friend. She growled, a distinctly draconic sound. "Let me go." Behind her she could hear Nate talking to the girl.

"I'm Nate. My friends are going to find the key. They'd probably move a little faster if they didn't think I was in danger."

"If I let you go, you'll run," the girl said.

"Nah, then you might yell and wake Stanley." Nate glanced over his shoulder. *"I've got this. Get the key so we can unlock these chains. She looks like she needs a doctor."*

Claire allowed Roy to tug her out of the room. *"What if Stanley doesn't have the key?"*

"You should be asking what if he does have it. Trying to get the key will wake him." Roy glanced towards the exit. *"Wait here. Let me know if Stanley wakes."* He strode towards the stairs and was up them and out the door in seconds, closing it behind him.

Claire glanced towards Nate once more before she went to Stanley's door, pressing her ear against it. Everything was silent. After a couple of minutes she heard him roll over, his hand connecting with something. Probably the wall or the bedside cabinet.

She held her breath. He continued to sleep. "*What are you doing, Roy?*" Standing around waiting was worse than getting in a fight. At least then she'd have been doing something.

"*I won't be long.*"

She managed not to growl. Barely. That hadn't answered her question. When everything remained quiet on the other side of the door, she listened at the other doors. They were silent too, the rooms smelling empty. She smiled wryly. That wasn't a thought she'd ever expected to have. Returning to Stanley's door, she froze. There was the rustling of bedding followed by someone yawning.

"*He's getting up.*" She stepped to the side of the door when she heard footsteps coming towards her. "*Roy? Nate? Stanley is out of bed.*"

"*Hide in one of the other rooms,*" Roy said.

"*What are you doing, Roy?*" She slipped into the room next to Stanley's closing the door behind her. "*And get out of that room, Nate. Do you want to be caught?*"

"*Liana won't let me go. Doesn't believe Stanley will check on her,*" Nate said.

"*Liana?*" Claire pressed her ear against the wall separating her from Stanley. Was he getting dressed? She heard a door close. At least Stanley wasn't in the room with the weapons. Although that didn't mean he was unarmed.

"*The dragon girl. She's only our age. We can't desert her,*" Nate said.

"*Don't trust anything a dragon says. She could be a lot older than she looks,*" Roy warned.

"*She said she was unplanned. All her siblings were more than fifty years older than her.*"

"*Were?*" Claire remained pressed against the wall, trying to figure out what Stanley was doing.

"*Tobiah led the group who killed them.*"

Claire had no idea what to say and was almost relieved to hear Stanley open his door and step into the hallway. "*Stanley's left his room. Where are you, Roy?*"

"*Upstairs. Stay out of sight.*"

She moved to the door and pressed her ear against it, fear racing through her. "*We left the hallway door open. He will check on Liana.*"

"What are you doing here?" Stanley demanded.

Claire's hand was on the door handle when Roy spoke.

"*Ask him where I am. Pretend I haven't come home.*"

"Where's Roy? What did you do with him?" Nate demanded.

Claire smiled at how convincing he sounded. Her

hand remained on the door handle, her body tense, ready to run to Nate's rescue.

"I have no idea what you're talking about. You. Let him go," Stanley ordered.

"Why should I?" Liana demanded. "If I snap his neck you won't get any answers from him. I bet he couldn't hold out against your methods."

Claire was across the hall and slamming Stanley against the bars of Liana's cell before she could think. The girl let go of Nate to grab Stanley, her arm slipping through the bars to pull him back against them, one arm across his neck.

"Don't kill him." Nate tried to loosen Liana's grip.

"He deserves to die. He's a Knight." Liana emphasised the last word, filling it with hate. "They all deserve to die."

Stanley struggled to escape, pulling at Liana's arm, gasping for breath. As much as she hated to, Claire tried to help him.

Roy strode into the room. "He's ours. Let him go. We have first claim on him."

"If I can't have Tobiah, I'll start with this one." Liana continued to pull Stanley back against the bars.

"Step back," Roy ordered Claire and Nate.

About to protest, Claire stepped away when he said the words 'trust me' in her and Nate's minds.

"You kill him and we'll leave you in that cell. Let him go and we'll look for a key." Roy held a damp cloth in his hand, pulling Stanley towards him when Liana let him go and he dropped to the floor. He pressed the cloth over Stanley's nose. The man went still.

Claire wrinkled her nose. "What's that?" She gestured towards the cloth Roy tossed in one corner.

"What they used on us. Sorry it took me so long to find it." Roy patted Stanley down, taking a phone from one of his pockets before he stood and faced Liana. "We're going to have a look for the key. You can yell all you want, but there's only us here."

Liana grabbed the bars. "Don't leave me here."

Claire paused in the doorway, having followed Roy and Nate. "We won't."

"You expect me to trust you? I don't even know what you are. What kind of dragon also smells like rodents?"

Claire smiled. "A unique one."

Roy continued along the hallway. *"I'll search upstairs. You handle Liana."*

Nate looked back in the room, over Claire's shoulder, grinning. "A freak of nature." His grin faded. "It doesn't matter what you've done. You don't deserve what they've done to you. We'll turn this place upside down if we have to, but we will find the key and will let you out."

"Do you promise?" Liana sounded younger than her age.

"Yes." Claire spoke at the same time as Nate, turning to him with a smile. "I'll search Stanley's room. You start on one of the others."

It took them nearly an hour to find the key, having found numerous ones that didn't fit the lock during the process. The key was in the cleaning supplies cupboard, which appeared to have less bottles of bleach than last time. Claire's jaw tightened as she remembered Roy's explanation. How could they have tortured Liana? And they obviously had from the look of her.

Roy stood out of reach of Liana, the cell door open. "Promise me you won't do anything rash."

"Let me out and I won't harm any of you," Liana spoke through gritted teeth.

"That wasn't what I said." Roy remained where he was.

"You're not going to leave her here," Nate said.

"I won't let her ruin our plans and put either of you in danger," Roy said.

Liana gestured towards Nate and Claire. "They promised."

Roy held up the key. "They don't have the key."

"Roy-" Claire broke off when he spoke in her mind.

"We can't trust her. But she will abide by her promise. As long as we word things properly. All dragons have to abide by their word. It's one of their few laws."

"We can't stand around here all day." Nate glanced at Stanley. "He'll eventually wake and anyone could arrive." He took a step towards Liana. "They kidnapped Claire and Roy because they want another person dead. A person they expected to trade themselves in exchange for Roy. I don't think they had any plans to let Claire go. We're trying to figure out a way to keep ourselves safe. All you need to do is promise not to ruin our plans."

"You're human. You wouldn't understand. There's no such thing as safe. The only thing you can do is take revenge."

Nate grinned. "Should I find it encouraging that you didn't say the word human with the same hate as you say the word Knight?"

Roy held up the key again. "Promise. And I'll unlock the chains."

Chapter Nineteen

Claire caught a glimpse of something in Liana's eyes. Fear? A moment of vulnerability? She wasn't sure. "Where will you go when you leave here?"

"That's none of your business."

"Have you got somewhere to go?" Nate asked.

Roy sighed. "She isn't someone in need of protecting. She's a dragon, capable of looking after herself. They're trained to believe in survival of the fittest."

"They?" Liana demanded of Roy. "Don't you mean 'us'? You're a dragon too. I can smell it."

"I wasn't raised a dragon."

"What were you raised as?"

Claire didn't know if she should stop Roy from telling Liana, especially with the way the girl felt about Knights.

Roy smiled fleetingly. "That is none of your business."

Nate laughed, holding up his hands when Liana and Roy both glared at him. "We're wasting time. What will it hurt to promise not to ruin our plans?"

"I want Tobiah. He needs to die." Anger flashed in Liana's eyes.

"For all we know he's already dead," Claire muttered.

"What happened?" Liana demanded.

"I attacked him." Claire tried not to remember that moment, but the image was etched into her brain. "There was a lot of blood." Attacking the wyvern had been far easier than attacking a human. Even one trying to kill her.

"Are you going to kill him?" Liana asked.

Before Claire could tell her 'no', Roy spoke.

"I'll do whatever it takes to protect Claire."

Liana grinned. "You might not have been raised a dragon, but that hasn't stopped you from being one. Dragons always protect what's theirs."

Claire didn't have the chance to say she belonged to no one. Roy spoke before she could.

"Last chance." He started to put the key in a pocket.

"Fine!"

"I need the words. Give me your promise," Roy said.

"I promise not to ruin your plans to protect your mate from Stanley and Tobiah, but when you're done, I will go after him. Tobiah needs to pay for the lives he took from me."

"You let Liana out. I'll put Stanley in the car." Roy gave the key to Claire, taking the car key from her. "Clean Liana up a bit before you bring her outside. It's daylight." He dragged Stanley upright and put him over his shoulder.

"What about what we came for?" Nate asked while Claire unlocked the cell door.

"We took too long." Roy stepped into the hallway. "I also don't think it's here." He continued towards the exit.

Claire looked up from the chains she was unlocking, at the sound of Roy's retreating footsteps, looking at Nate. "Take the blanket off Stanley's bed and cover him up before Roy takes him outside."

Nate hesitated.

Claire looked over at him with a smile. "We'll be okay. I can call if we need help."

Nate grinned. "Make sure you do. Don't keep all the fun to yourself." He strode from the room.

Liana watched him go. "He should have been a dragon. He thinks a lot like one."

Claire looked at the girl for a moment. Had she sounded disappointed? "He wouldn't argue that." Once the chains were off Liana, she pocketed the key and gestured towards the doorway. "Let's get you cleaned up and out of here."

"I need to find my weapons first." Liana attempted to stride out of the cell, but staggered, grabbing hold of the bars.

Claire tried to put an arm around the girl's waist. "Come on."

Liana pulled away from her. "I don't need your help. I'm not weak."

"I never said you were." A closer look at Liana showed a tremble in her hands and her jaw clenched tight like she struggled with something. Probably pain. Claire stepped out of the cell. "It's okay to ask for help when you're injured."

"What kind of dragon are you?" Liana brushed past Claire, her steps unsteady.

"I'll let you know when I figure it out." She grinned at the girl, the grin fading when Liana didn't return it. "What do your weapons look like?"

Liana grabbed hold of her forearm. "Don't show

weakness. There are those who'll pounce on it and tear you to shreds."

She started to argue the words, stopping when she realised Liana believed them. "Why warn me?"

"I owe you for helping me escape."

"No you don't."

"You think my life is worthless? You want nothing in return for it?"

She felt out of her depth and wished Roy was there to help her. "Only your promise."

"My life is worth more than that."

"We are talking lives. I don't want to end up dead."

Liana gave a single nod. "A life for a life. It's a deal." She took Claire's hand, shaking it. Letting go, she looked up and down the hallway. "A sword, two daggers and a wrist sheath." Liana entered the closest room.

Claire stared after her for a moment. Who carried around those types of weapons? An image of Roy and his daggers came to her. Obviously more people than she realised. "There are a couple of swords in a room with a heap of guns." She led the way, opening the built-in wardrobe to show Liana.

"Mine." The girl strapped on the sword, slipping daggers into boots and buckling up the wrist sheath.

She took a phone off the bedside cabinet, slipping it into a pocket of her trousers.

Claire stared at her.

"Why are you looking at me like that?" Liana demanded.

"You look ready for battle." Another battle. The way the girl held herself made her look every bit a warrior. That was the way she wanted to look. Capable, able to take on anything no matter what she'd already faced.

"Good." Liana gave a single nod. "I'm always ready for battle."

Maybe she wasn't so far off that capable look. She was always ready for battle too. Or at least a fight. "I'll show you where the bathroom is." They'd barely stepped into the hallway when Roy spoke in their minds.

"*Wayne pulled up out the front. Get out the back. He has Tobiah with him.*"

"*Get out of my head,*" Liana ordered.

"*There's no time to escape. Wayne didn't wait for Tobiah. He's already inside,*" Roy said.

Claire closed the door of the room they'd left. "*We'll hide in Stanley's room. They shouldn't look in there.*" She crossed the distance in a couple of seconds, closing the door before she'd finished speaking. "*Are you both safe? What about Stanley?*"

"*Claire, get out of that room. Wayne told Tobiah he was getting Stanley to help him to his room,*" Roy said.

She reached for the door handle, lowering her hand when she heard the footsteps coming down the stairs. "*It's too late.*" She glanced around the room. There were no hiding places.

"Are you going to panic?" Liana demanded, her voice a whisper.

She slowed her breathing. There was nothing she could do about her racing heart. "No." Opening the built-in wardrobe, she pushed the clothes to one side, stepping into it. "Hurry up." She gestured towards the space beside her, closing the door once Liana was inside.

"*Claire? What is happening?*" Roy asked. "*Do you need us to come for you?*"

"*No. You'll get caught,*" Claire said to them.

"*Don't you get caught,*" Nate said.

Wayne knocked on the door. "Stanley. Get out here and help." There was a moment of silence. "Stanley! What are you doing in bed? You should be up by now." The door swung open, footsteps crossing the room.

"*He's in the room with us,*" Claire told Roy. "*I can

hear him looking under the bed. Or at least that's what I guess he's doing."

"I'll ring him," Roy said.

"How do you have his number?" Liana demanded.

"I have Stanley's phone."

Wayne's phone began to ring before Roy had finished speaking. "Where are you?" There was a moment's pause. "What have you done with him?"

Claire strained to hear what Roy said, surprised when she heard him speak. His voice was faint, but loud enough for her to follow the conversation.

"If you want him back you need to leave me out of it. And the girl that was with me. And you're not to come after either of our families," Roy said.

Wayne laughed, a short, sharp sound that wasn't in the least humorous. "You can keep him. I'd rather have Amber. Fredrick doesn't care about Stanley and that's all I care about."

Tobiah stepped into the room, his breath laboured. "What is going on? Where's Stanley? How many times have I got to tell you not to leave my cousin behind?"

Wayne hung up the phone. "You're meant to be resting. The doctor said you need to take it easy for a few weeks."

Claire listened to them walk away, arguing about Stanley.

"*He hung up on me,*" Roy said.

"*I know. You rang the wrong one. Stanley is Tobiah's cousin.*" Claire grabbed hold of Liana when she began to slide down the wall. Worry rushed through her when the girl didn't protest. She felt dampness and feared it was blood. They had to get out of here before Liana bled to death.

"*I'll call him later, when you're out of there,*" Roy said.

Should she tell him that Liana might have collapsed? He'd be at her side in minutes. Caught seconds later. "*It might take us a bit to get past Wayne. Quiet a minute. They've stopped arguing about Stanley. I need to focus on what they're saying.*" She struggled to hold Liana up, the girl seeming to grow heavier by the second.

"Find Stanley. You want me to stay in bed, then you find my cousin. If he's not back by morning I'll be getting out of bed and looking for him myself," Tobiah said. "And check on the dragon. We need to know why she attacked and who else might be after us."

"We have to focus on what's important. Getting back in good with Fredrick. Giving him Amber will do that. Forget Stanley. He's already caused you enough problems. You wouldn't be trying to make good with Fredrick if you hadn't made your cousin a Knight Mage," Wayne said.

"My brothers are gone. Stanley is all the family I have left." Tobiah breathed in sharply, the sound accompanied by the swish of bed linen being moved.

"He's not worth worrying about. You're better off with no family," Wayne said.

"Check on the dragon. Keep your opinions to yourself. I was warned against helping you. That I'd be better off finding my own way to make peace with Fredrick."

"Who warned you?" Wayne demanded.

"It doesn't matter. But it's starting to look like they were right."

Chapter Twenty

Claire bit back an exclamation of surprise when Liana drew away, her body colliding with the wall, the impact softened by the clothes pushed to the end of the hanging rail. "*Quiet.*" She tried to focus on Liana, not wanting Roy and Nate to wonder what was going on.

Footsteps sounded in the hall, followed by curses and Wayne running back to Tobiah. "She's gone. They took her too. Or at least someone did."

"They must have her. It'd be too much of a coincidence someone else breaking in on the same day. Bring me my phone. I need to talk to them," Tobiah ordered.

"Here. I'll be back shortly. We need more people."

Wayne's scent vanished from the building and Claire guessed he'd used a caged Pliethin. "*We have to go before he brings help.*" She opened the door and grabbed a black, large shirt off a coat hanger. *"Put this on. It'll help hide some of the more noticeable injuries."*

"What is going on?" Nate demanded.

"Who is bringing back help?" Roy asked.

Claire nearly groaned. Obviously her words hadn't been sent only to Liana. *"We'll be out there shortly. Have the car started and be ready to go."* Once Liana had put on the shirt and buttoned it, she put an arm around her.

"Do you know why Tobiah is ringing Stanley's phone?" Roy asked.

"Yeah. He misses his cousin. Keep him busy." Claire worried about how badly Liana was hurt when she continued to lean against her. She heard Tobiah demand to know where his cousin was as they continued up the stairs. Reaching the top she struggled to support Liana and open the door. Letting her fall from the top of a flight of stairs sounded like an extremely bad idea.

Stepping into the kitchen, her attention was caught by the caged Pliethin on the table. She'd taken three steps towards it when Wayne came out of the Void on the other side of the table, an unknown Knight with him.

Wayne remained immobile for a few seconds before throwing himself towards the table.

Liana tugged Claire with her, grabbed the caged Pliethin off the table, slid her arm around Claire and plunged her fingers into the cage. She dragged them into the Void, the kitchen viewed as if through a fog. "Don't let go of me or you'll be lost in here."

"Why didn't you use the Void to escape the moment we let you go?"

"I didn't have the energy. Pliethins are pure energy. Mages aren't the only ones who can use them. Golds can too."

One of the conversations she'd had with Roy about Gold Warrior dragons being the only dragons able to use the Void came back to her. "Don't Golds have castles? How could anyone get your family if they were in a castle?"

"They came out of the Void and my family weren't that important. Not important enough to be able to afford the stones that keep dragons and mages from remaining in the Void." Liana took a step towards the front of the house. "We have to keep moving. If I pass out we'll be out of the Void and they'll be able to capture us."

"We'll never get out of here this way." The air in the Void was heavier than she'd expected. She'd only ever spent a few seconds going from one destination to the other, not walking around in it. Her phone vibrated, indicating an incoming call.

"Leave it. You don't have time to answer. We have to get out of here." Liana spoke through gritted teeth.

Claire tried to move faster. It was impossible. A glance behind her showed more Knight Mages coming out of the Void. "Why can't they see us when they're in the Void? Or hear us."

"It doesn't work like that. Stop talking and keep moving."

She wanted to say she hadn't stopped moving, but at the speed they were walking it was a little hard to argue that fact. "I really need to learn how to do this." If she could do it. She could feel the tremble in Liana's body with how the girl leaned against her. She managed to suppress the words before she did something stupid like ask how Liana was doing.

It seemed to take forever before they were outside. Relief washed through her, vanishing a moment later when they came out of the Void, Liana collapsing against her. "*Nate!*" She called for him mentally, the car only metres from her, Roy in the driver's seat.

Nate threw open the car door, running towards them, scooping up Liana. "What happened?"

She clutched the caged Pliethin to her chest, having grabbed it when Liana brought them out of the Void before collapsing. "I'll tell you once we're out of here." Reaching the car, she held open the back door so Nate could put Liana next to Stanley, who was wrapped in a blanket. She slid in next to her, keeping the unconscious girl upright. "We can't go to my place. Someone is probably watching it. Or at least watching your place."

Roy drove off the moment Nate was in the car. "I called Amos. We'll meet him at the industrial shed."

Nate turned in his seat to look at Liana. "She's bleeding."

"What are we going to do with her?" The girl looked younger than seventeen now she wasn't glaring fiercely at them.

"Patch her up and let her go," Roy said.

"What if she has nowhere to go?" Pain arrowed through her at the thought of losing her entire family. She didn't know if she'd be able to do anything other than cry. "Why would Knights kill her family?"

"I don't know," Roy said. "Once I would have said it was because they'd killed humans, now…" His voice trailed off. "These days it's hard to know who is in the wrong."

Roy's words brought silence. Claire alternated between looking out the window and checking Liana. Occasionally she checked the caged Pliethin that remained on her lap. She tried not to think about the fact they had everything they needed for Nate to try and become a dragon.

Amos met them at the front gate, throwing Stanley over his shoulder and taking him inside the apartment. Claire followed Roy, who carried Liana, Nate beside her. She noticed he kept glancing at the caged Pliethin. She stopped not far inside the apartment when Amos straightened after tying Stanley's hands and feet together and stalked towards her.

"What did you think you were doing?" He gestured towards Liana and Stanley, both unconscious.

Roy was in front of Claire in seconds. "Coming up with solutions. Tobiah wants Stanley. I spoke to him. He's willing to agree not to go after us if we return his cousin. I couldn't get him to agree not to go after Amber, but he won't use us against her."

"What about Stanley and Wayne? Will they agree to the deal?" Amos demanded.

"Tobiah said he'd get Stanley to agree, but he couldn't do anything about Wayne. Not that it will matter. Those currently helping Wayne are Tobiah's people," Roy said.

"He'll find others to help him. Wayne won't give up. He never gives up."

Roy nodded at his uncle's words. "Which means we'll only have him to deal with."

"A pity we can't get it done before my dad comes home tomorrow," Claire said.

Nate grinned. "He won't be home until mid morning. We've got plenty of time."

Amos faced Nate, a finger pointed at him. "You will not rush in and get Roy killed. This isn't a game." He turned to Roy. "Organise a time and place and I'll return Stanley. If anything happened to you, Eliza would kill me."

Roy nodded. "I turned Stanley's phone off in case Tobiah can use it to track us down. I'll leave it a couple of hours before I contact him again. I wouldn't want to seem desperate."

"We aren't desperate," Amos stated.

Roy shrugged.

Amos pointed a finger at him. "We are never desperate. There's always something we can do." He didn't wait for an answer, striding outside and shutting the door.

Claire hurried to the door and looked out. Amos was gone. Closing the door, she leaned against it.

"What now?" She continued to hold the caged Pliethin.

"I want to become a dragon," Nate said.

"Are you sure?" Roy asked. "If it works, there's no going back. Life will always be dangerous and there's likely to be numerous battles in your future."

Claire laughed. "If you were trying to talk him out of it you came up with the wrong examples."

Nate grinned. "We've got everything but a concrete floor. And surely that can't be too hard to find."

"Right through that door." Claire pointed to the door that led into the rest of the building.

"Then what are we waiting for?" Nate demanded.

Roy took out a small, amber coloured bottle from his pocket and grabbed a cloth from under the sink. He opened the bottle and held the cloth to the opening before tipping it up.

"What are you doing?" She came away from the door.

"Making sure Stanley and Liana don't wake up while Nate and I are unconscious." Roy held the cloth to Stanley's nose before moving to Liana.

"But she's-"

Roy interrupted Claire. "We don't know anything about her. We won't be able to help you." He left the bottle and cloth on the bench and took out a small jar, tipping some of the content into a glass he took from the cupboard.

Claire moved closer to the bench, along with Nate. "What is that?"

Roy added water to the glass and swirled the contents. "Dragon bone." He downed the contents.

Claire shuddered. "Isn't that like being a cannibal or something?"

"Dragons are different." Roy rinsed the glass out and turned it upside down, leaving it on the side of the sink. He picked up the cloth. "Use this on Liana in a couple of hours to make sure she doesn't wake up while we're out. Put a bit more of it on the cloth first. Only hold it to her nose for a couple of seconds. You don't want her unconscious too long. You don't need to worry about Stanley. He'll stay under a lot longer."

"You can't do that to her," Nate said. "It's not right."

"You'd rather leave Claire unprotected?" Roy handed the cloth to Claire before he moved the television cabinet out of the way and set up the sofa bed.

"Of course I don't want to leave her unprotected, but…" Nate shrugged.

"This is best. They'll both be safe here. No one

can find us in this room." Roy sat on the edge of the bed. "Lie down, Nate." He took the cloth from Claire when she came close.

"What's it like?" Nate nodded to the cloth as he lay on the bed.

"Like nothing," Claire said. "One minute you're awake, the next you're waking up with some time missing."

Roy pressed the cloth over Nate's nose. "Breathe deep." He handed the cloth to Claire when Nate's eyes closed and his breathing evened out. "Count to two. I'll be awake before Nate." He lay down. "We don't want to use as much as we were given last time."

"Why not?"

"It isn't necessary. It'd keep us under too long."

Chapter Twenty-One

Claire sat beside Roy, smiling. "Thank you for doing this."

"It might help my family too."

"Would it be so bad to let people know you're dragons?"

Roy smiled. "We're Knights."

Claire chuckled. "Yeah, I know. You've told me that often enough. But surely being Knights doesn't mean you can't be dragons too."

Roy took her hand. "The two are mortal enemies. Trust me. Being a dragon is the worst thing possible for a Knight. I've tried to avoid being one my entire life."

"Sorry I forced you to change forms."

Roy remained silent for a moment. He squeezed her hand. "Time to put me to sleep."

She leaned forward and brushed her lips across his.

"I'll see you soon." Straightening, she pressed the cloth against his nose, counting to two before she removed it, continuing to hold his hand. She stared at him, his face relaxed, his breathing unchanged. How did he manage to remain calm when half the time things were going crazy? She needed to figure out how to do that.

Reluctantly rising to her feet, she placed the cloth on the kitchen bench and set the timer on her phone so she didn't forget to use the cloth on Liana again. Her gaze was drawn to each of the unconscious bodies, a grin forming. The situation would be a little difficult to explain if anyone burst into the apartment.

Her thoughts returned to earlier that day when they'd broken into the house. It would have been easier if she'd been able to turn into a mouse. Taking a deep breath, she tried to focus on changing. No matter how hard she tried, her body only wanted to become a dragon. She wouldn't allow the change to occur. Why couldn't she turn into a mouse? So they were tiny and vulnerable. That didn't mean she couldn't change back to human or dragon form if she needed to protect herself. But it didn't matter. She couldn't become a mouse. Sighing, she checked the time. It had been over an hour.

She sat on the edge of the bed, looking from Roy

to Nate and back again. They looked peaceful. Were they doing the right thing trying to turn Nate into a dragon? It only took her a couple of seconds to decide they were. She wasn't about to ditch her best friend and being a human around dragons didn't seem like the safest option. The sound of the door opening had her on her feet and facing it in seconds, ready to protect her companions.

"What happened to contacting Tobiah in a couple of hours?"

She shrugged. "Plans change."

"Where's Stanley's phone?"

"Probably in one of Roy's pockets."

Amos strode to the bed, checking pockets and taking the phone from one. "Tell him I'll sort it out. Eliza wants him to stay out of it." He gestured towards Nate. "She's not going to be impressed with this." He turned away and picked up Stanley, tossing him over his shoulder. "Call me if there's a problem. Don't get him killed."

She was standing there, staring after him minutes after he'd left. What if they'd wanted to sort it out? Not that she had any idea how to return someone that had been kidnapped. She paced the limited floor space. How did one know the person they were negotiating with wasn't going to try something?

Different scenarios filled her mind with all the things that could have gone wrong. Was she ready for any of this? For a moment she wanted her dad. She pushed that feeling aside. She was capable. Had been looking after herself for more than a year.

Her alarm went off, causing her heart to race. Reminding herself it was only an alarm, and nothing else, she dealt with Liana. Crouching beside the girl she stared at her, feeling like she should apologise. At least Liana's wounds no longer bled. Worried about how uncomfortable it must be on the floor, she took one of the pillows out of the cupboard and lifted her head. Would using a wet washer to clean off some of the blood wake the girl? In the end she left her alone, returning to the bed so she could sit beside Roy. She took hold of his hand. How much longer would it be until he woke?

As if he heard her question, Roy's eyes opened. "Did you sit by me the entire time?"

Claire grinned. "I don't think I know how to sit still that long."

Roy laughed softly, glancing at Nate when he sat up. "Where's Stanley?"

"How could you tell he wasn't here?" She looked at the location where the Knight had been. Roy hadn't even checked that spot.

"I can't smell him."

She grinned again. "That makes him sound like he never takes a bath."

Roy smiled fleetingly, moving off the bed, drawing her up with him. "What happened?"

"Amos took him. Your mum isn't happy. She didn't want you to have anything to do with the negotiations. More than likely she doesn't want you to have anything to do with making dragons."

Roy drew her close, his arms sliding around her waist. "She's always been overprotective. Probably the dragon in her. They can be fierce about what they think is theirs."

His hands were warm against her back when she slid her arms around his neck. "They? Don't you mean we? You're a dragon too."

"I try not to be."

"I don't think it's that simple. Even I can smell dragon on your skin. Faint, less noticeable than on Amos, but I can smell it."

"I know. It's stronger since I held the Pliethin."

"Is that a problem?" She met his gaze, waiting for his answer. It didn't come immediately.

"I don't know."

"Will it get worse if you hold a second Pliethin?"

Again he didn't answer immediately. "I know very

little about dragons." He smiled wryly. "Other than how to kill them."

Claire grinned. "That's not exactly the kind of information we need right now."

"I'm afraid I can't help you." He paused a moment. "There are people I could ask, but that would mean risking Amber putting herself in danger. That'd be a poor way to thank her for all the times she's saved my life."

"Then I guess we figure it out as we go along." Pretty much the way she normally lived her life. A grin formed again. "Could be fun."

"Could be dangerous."

She nodded. "More than likely." Before he could say anything else, she pressed her lips against his, moving as close to him as possible.

"Hope you plan to keep things PG. I don't need to be mentally scarred for life."

Claire faced Nate, keeping one arm around Roy. "You woke sooner than I expected. I was going to see if there was a marker pen and draw on your face."

"A moustache and bushy eyebrows?" Nate stumbled out of bed. "Wow, don't think I'm properly with it yet."

"As if I'd do anything as ordinary as that. I was thinking of a Frankenstein's monster look. Patched up face and exaggerated stitches." Letting go of Roy, she moved forward to put an arm around Nate.

Roy went to Nate's other side, slipping an arm around his waist. "Sit down for a minute."

Nate sat on the stool, grinning at Claire. "That look'd be okay."

"Guess I can forget that plan. You're not meant to be happy when someone draws on your face while you're asleep."

Roy took a step back, looking from one to the other. "If you're worried, you don't have to go through with this."

Claire took hold of Nate's hand, holding it tightly. "It doesn't hurt." She grinned. "At least not much. Just like ripping off a band aid."

"In that case, we better get it over and done with." Nate stood up unsteadily. "Don't they say to do it quick and it hurts less?"

"I think it's a myth." Claire continued to hold Nate's hand, looking to Roy. She frowned. "Are you okay? You don't look all that good."

"Dragon bone."

"You're going to have to stop with the answers that don't explain anything." She reached out and rested her palm against his cheek, continuing to hold Nate's hand.

"Dragons can consume any part of another dragon other than the bones. Well, legally they're not meant to eat the heart as that dramatically increases their lifespan, but it won't make them ill."

Claire made a face. "Okay. Let's not think about that anymore." Stepping away from both of them, she collected the caged Pliethin and headed to the far door. She stopped to look back at them. "Are we doing this?"

Nate nodded before he joined her at the door, Roy following him. They stepped into the larger area, closing the door behind them. Reaching the middle of the room, Roy removed his shirt so he stood in dragon leather trousers and Nate stripped down to his boxers in case he changed form. If their experiment worked.

"You'll need more dragon blood." Roy cut his hand, doing the same to Nate's hand when he held it out.

Nate hissed when their palms met. "This is getting to be a habit." He lowered his hand after a few seconds.

Claire held out the caged Pliethin. "I broke the cage and held onto the Pliethin while the cage hung around my wrist." She went through each step once more, both boys nodding at her words. Eventually she fell silent, looking from one to the other. "Are you ready?"

Roy nodded.

Nate didn't answer immediately. "Almost." He took some black fur from the pocket of his jeans that lay on the concrete floor and tucked it into the waistband of his boxers.

"What is that?" Claire pointed at the black fur, pretty certain she already knew.

"Cat fur."

"Why?" She glared at the tuft. "You're not going to become a cat."

"We live in a city. What else would blend into the surroundings? Besides, cats are awesome."

"They also eat mice."

Nate grinned. "Guess you better be nice to me in future."

She hit his arm. "You're not choosing a cat."

"It's logical."

"No it's not."

Roy stepped between them. "He'll still be himself, once he gets the hang of changing. He won't eat you."

She faced Roy. "He better not. It's bad enough Bub thinks I'm his next meal."

Nate laughed.

She hit his arm again. It didn't stop his laughter. Her eyes narrowed and she took the caged Pliethin from him. "You going to apologise or am I keeping my Pliethin?"

Nate continued to grin, stepping closer. "You wouldn't."

She put it behind her back. "Wouldn't I?" She spun to face Roy when he took the Pliethin from her. "Whose side are you on?"

"Neither. Liana won't stay asleep forever. If this works we can't share the process with everyone." Roy held the caged Pliethin out to Nate. "Ready?"

"Yes." Nate smashed the cage against the concrete floor. It cracked open. The Pliethin trying to escape. He grabbed hold of it, the cage dangling from his wrist.

Chapter Twenty-Two

Claire stepped back, worried she'd get in the way. She watched as Roy took hold of Nate's hand. Both were tall. One wiry, the other solid. Both were muscular. They tensed. Roy took the Pliethin from Nate, continuing to hold his hand. Both of them gasped, heads flung back, pain etched across their features. She clasped her hands to keep from running forward to help.

Nate cried out, stumbling backwards when Roy let go of him to change forms. Nate's mouth opened when Roy's ebony scales became bathed in the gold light from the Pliethin.

Claire came forward to wrap an arm around Nate's waist. "It's an amazing sight, isn't it?"

"Yes." Nate's word was as soft as hers had been. He leaned heavily against her. "I feel odd."

"In a good or bad way?"

Before Nate could answer, Roy became human again, sinking to his knees, his gaze on the Pliethin. "I'm sorry." He opened his hand and the now grey Pliethin rose and vanished.

"Is it okay?" Nate stumbled forward, nearly falling.

Claire grabbed him. "The other Pliethin did that too."

"It'll regain its power and return to this world another day." Roy slowly got to his feet, breathing in deeply. "It worked."

"How can you tell?" Claire asked.

"Smell him."

Nate grinned. "Sounds like an insult."

She turned her head, breathing deeply. "Dragon."

Roy nodded. "And house cat."

"House cat sounds rather tame. I was thinking tomcat. Or alley cat." Nate pulled away from Claire. "How do I change?"

"You want to be careful. Tomcats tend to get neutered." She tried not to smile, but couldn't resist.

The door leading into the apartment opened and they turned to face Liana. She frowned, her gaze stopping on Nate. "How did you hide the scent of dragon earlier?"

"I was-"

Roy interrupted Nate. "An experiment we're struggling to replicate."

Liana strode towards them. "That'd be useful. I want to learn how to do it too."

Claire met her partway. "How do you feel? I was worried you'd bleed to death back at the house."

Liana lifted a shoulder. "I'm harder to kill than that."

"There's a bathroom if you want to get cleaned up." She took several steps towards the open door, wondering if Liana had noticed the broken Pliethin cage.

"I found the bathroom."

Amos came through the still open door. "What are you all doing in here? Are you trying to get caught? Get back in the apartment and shut the door. The stones won't keep you hidden if you don't use them."

Claire hurried past Amos. "Nate needs dragon leather trousers."

"What do you think I am?" Amos pointed a finger at Claire when she opened her mouth to speak. "I would be careful what answer you give."

Nate entered the apartment, his clothes in his arms. "I'd borrow a pair of Roy's, but they'd probably end up around my ankles." He grinned. "Some people might be offended. Not sure why though."

Claire elbowed him. "Idiot." The word was said with its usual fondness.

Amos pointed first at Roy, then at Nate. "You pair will stay here." He turned to Liana. "I don't care where you go." He faced Claire. "And you are going home."

She wanted to argue even though she did need to go home. Her dad would expect her to be there when he arrived tomorrow.

"I didn't ask to be brought here." Liana headed for the front door.

Claire hurried after her. "Wait. Let me give you my number in case you need to call me." She looked the girl up and down. "And maybe you better come back to my place and get cleaned up. I can lend you some clothes."

"Why would you do that?" Liana demanded.

She was confused. "Because it's the right thing to do."

Liana shook her head. "The right thing to do would be to let me survive on my own. Only the fittest survive."

Roy joined them by the front door. "That doesn't mean you have to do it alone. It's okay to have allies."

"Roy." There was a warning in Amos' voice.

Roy smiled wryly. "I can't offer much since I have

little of my own. My family wouldn't back me in offering you their help. But if it's something I can offer, then you're welcome to it."

"How will I know if it's something you can offer?" Liana asked.

Roy's smile became a grin. "Ask."

Nate joined them, his jeans back on, his shirt in his hand. "I'll give you my number too. Ring anytime. Even if you're only looking for someone to go out and have a bit of fun with."

"Do any of you have a brain?" Amos demanded.

Claire turned to him. "Of course we do." She paused a second. "Can you bring Liana to my place once you've dropped me there? And what happened with Stanley?"

"No and we're negotiating the terms."

"Yes and how long will that take?" Claire asked.

"I don't need to go to your place." Liana tried to push past Claire.

She stopped her with a smile. "Of course you do. You're welcome anytime. Although if my dad is there, don't let him know what we are. He knows nothing."

"You have a human father?" Liana sneered the word 'human'.

"Yes." She didn't feel the need to apologise. Liana

would eventually learn that humans weren't that bad. She turned to Amos. "It'll take you a few seconds to bring Liana to my place."

Amos pushed past all of them and stepped outside, grabbing Claire's arm to drag her out with him.

Before she could protest, he was leaving her in her laundry, returning a few seconds later with Liana. He pointed a warning finger at Claire. "Leave Roy out of it. He doesn't need any of the trouble you'll cause."

He was gone before she could argue. She wasn't the one who'd caused the trouble. It was Knight Mages long before she'd met Roy.

"He doesn't like you much."

Claire grinned. "I don't think he likes me at all."

Liana stared at her a moment. "You're wrong. He likes you a bit, but it's reluctant. He has a certain amount of respect for you."

"Why would you say that?"

"He brought me here, didn't he?"

Claire shrugged, not sure that meant anything. More than likely it was because he was fed up arguing with her.

"His eyes don't have the hate in them that they do when he looks at me."

"I'm sorry. He-"

Liana interrupted. "It's as it should be. I'm the

enemy. You shouldn't be helping me. We have no allies in common. You should have left me in that cell. But I understand now. You don't know any better. It's the fault of your human parent. Your dragon parent should have known better than to let your human parent help raise you."

"Ah…" She had no idea what to say. Both of her parents were human. "I'll show you where the bathroom is and get a change of clothes for you."

While Liana washed, she made a late lunch. They ate it silently. When they'd finished, Claire gave Liana her phone number and offered the use of her room so the girl could have a rest. She looked exhausted.

"There's nothing wrong with me."

Claire managed not to smile at the indignant words. "I just assumed you'd had no sleep. I mean who would sleep when kept in a cell. It stands to reason you'd have been awake." She shrugged. "You don't have to rest if you don't want to. I've got to unpack some boxes that have been stacked in the spare room." She headed to the spare room, trying not to glance behind her when Liana followed. Ignoring the girl, she opened up the closest box.

After a few minutes, Liana spoke. "I might as well sleep. That way I can go hunting tonight."

"I don't mind." She glanced at Liana, focusing on her task when she would have preferred to ask what Liana planned to hunt. It was another couple of minutes before Liana wandered off. Claire kept unpacking, listening to Liana walk down the hallway and into her bedroom. The girl remained quiet and Claire grinned. It must be annoying always having to act invincible. Her grin faded. When would Liana have the chance to mourn her family?

She took a break an hour later and sent Roy a text to see how he was doing. He sent one back to say he and Nate were training with Amos. Putting her phone away, she returned to unpacking, not taking another break until Liana woke.

They had another silent meal, Liana rising from the table when she was finished. "Thank you." She gestured towards the table. "You didn't need to do all this."

"I know." Claire rose. "You can stay the night if you want."

Liana shook her head. "I have to go." She took a step back.

Claire grabbed hold of her arm. "You're welcome to return. My dad will be here around midmorning tomorrow. He'll be here for a week."

Liana pulled out of her light grip. "Why would you tell me that?"

"So you don't appear in front of him and surprise him."

"You gave me tactical information."

Claire grinned. "No. My dad is human. As if he'd be able to take on a dragon when he doesn't know they exist."

"Your mum should have taught him about our world instead of letting him come into it without knowing anything. That's dangerous." Liana vanished.

Claire stared at the place where the dragon girl had been. Surely she was wrong. It couldn't be that bad. Shaking her head, she looked at the dishes on the table. She'd return to unpacking once the kitchen was cleaned up.

Chapter Twenty-Three

The sound of her name being called had Claire sitting up, looking around in confusion. She was on the floor of the spare room, a box half unpacked in front of her. Groaning she rose to her feet, pushing her hair back from her face. She'd fallen asleep unpacking?

"Claire?" Heavy footsteps entered the hallway.

"In the spare room, Dad. I'm unpacking." She straightened her clothes, ran her fingers through her hair, then stepped into the hallway, trying to smile instead of giving into the tears that threatened to fall at the sight of him.

"Weren't you going to wait until I was home to continue with the unpacking?" He stopped in front of her, glancing in the room. "You're nearly done."

She shrugged. "I had nowhere for friends to stay."

Darrell smiled. "Friends or one friend in particular?"

She shrugged again, this time her smile coming easier. "I have more than one friend." Maybe they were more like acquaintances, but he'd made it sound like they didn't exist.

"I can set the spare bed up once I put my gear away. Then I'll fix that broken fence this arve."

"It's your first day back. There's no need to spend it getting all the jobs done. Setting up the bed will be enough for today."

"Didn't you hassle me every day before I left to fix that fence? That you were worried the dog would get out?" He glanced around. "Speaking of, where is the bloody nuisance?"

Shock ran through her. She'd forgotten all about Bubbles. "I let him out earlier. I'll go get him. He's getting better at not running off." She rushed past her dad, taking the phone from her pocket as she went. Stepping outside, she dialled Amos' phone number that he'd given her. "I need the dog. My dad is home."

Amos swore. "You couldn't have remembered last night?"

"Obviously not." There'd been other things to worry about. Like injured dragons, Knight Mages likely wanting her dead and Nate becoming a dragon. "Will you bring him to me or do I go next door and ask Eliza for him?" She'd never met Roy's mum and didn't want her first time to be asking for Bubbles. Actually, she wasn't sure she wanted to meet the woman who was extremely protective of her son. What would Eliza think of her?

"Make sure the laundry is clear."

She returned inside. Her dad was nowhere in sight. "It's all good."

Amos appeared in front of her, disconnecting the call and slipping his phone into a pocket before holding out the dog.

"Thank you." She barely got the words out, having taken the dog, when he disappeared. Bubbles tried to escape from her grip. "No you don't," she muttered. It didn't take her long to find her dad. He was in the kitchen, making coffee. "Here he is."

Darrell glanced at her, taking a second longer look, his gaze fixed on the dog. "Have you told your mother?"

"Ah, no."

"I guess that's one way of getting out of looking after him again."

A reluctant chuckle escaped. "It wasn't exactly planned."

"No wonder he hasn't been wandering. Probably worried about what you'll do next."

This time the chuckle came more easily. "Maybe."

She let Bubbles go, watching him as he scampered away. "I better shut some doors. He's not happy with me."

Once the doors were closed, she joined her dad for a late breakfast before the two of them finished the unpacking and set up the spare bed, pushing a bedside cabinet into place next to the single bed.

Claire straightened the doonah and stood back to survey the room. "That didn't take as long to finish as I thought it would." A check of her phone showed it wasn't yet lunch. Not that she was ready for more to eat after a late breakfast.

"Want to give me a hand to fix the fence?"

"Why don't we watch a movie? You've been working all week. Don't you want to relax for a bit?"

"What is the-" Darrell broke off his sentence to start again. "You're using the gap to visit next door. Didn't we agree you weren't going to meet the neighbours while I was gone?"

"Bubs introduced me."

"When are you going to introduce me to him?"

"Uhm…" She had no idea how she'd manage that. Not with Wayne looking for them. "I've got school this week."

"Today isn't over yet."

"Roy is out with Nate." It was kind of true. They

were in the same location. Or at least she supposed they were. She hadn't heard from either of them today.

"Is this another one who is going to be just a friend? You're not angling to date that older one, are you?"

"No and I hope not." Realising she'd answered the questions out of order, she said, "That was no to the second question."

"That's a relief, but how old is…" Darrell frowned. "Roy, was it?"

"He's eighteen. Basically my age."

"I want to meet him before I return to work. I don't like you hanging out with people I haven't met. And I want to meet his family too."

She wanted to protest. Did she really want him meeting Eliza? After all she'd heard about the woman she didn't want her anywhere near her dad. Or Amos near him. She doubted her dad would let her have anything to do with Roy once he met his family. She shrugged. "I'll see what I can do." She'd see what she could do to avoid them meeting each other. Hopefully meeting Roy would be enough for him. "About that movie."

Darrell shook his head. "You watch one if you want. I've got a few other things I should get done."

"Okay." She retreated to her bedroom, closing the door before she dropped onto her bed. She hadn't realised it would be so difficult. What did she tell her dad? Did she tell him anything? And if not, how would she keep being a dragon secret from him? Maybe Nate would know. She sent him a text telling him she needed to see him. Her phone rang almost instantly. Seeing the call was from Roy, it took her a few seconds to answer. "What's wrong?"

"That is what I was going to ask you. Nate got a message from you."

"You're sharing messages now?"

Roy chuckled. "He wanted to know if it was safe to go to your place."

"My dad wants to meet you."

"Is that what the problem is?"

It was her that laughed this time. "No. I just realised how hard it's going to be keeping it all from him. But he does want to meet you before he goes back to work. And your family."

"Is that what you wanted to talk to Nate about?"

"Not exactly. I wanted to know what he's decided to tell his family. I mean, we can't exactly tell them we're dragons."

"No, it'd cause other problems," Roy said.

Claire opened her mouth to ask what other

problems. Liana came out of the Void and she forgot what she wanted to say.

"They're in your neighbour's house." Liana gestured towards the front of the house. "The old one across from you."

"I have to ring you back," Claire told Roy.

"Wait. What's going on? Is that Li–"

She disconnected. "What were you doing over there?"

"You won't let me go after Tobiah, so I decided to do the next best thing. Go after Wayne for what he did to me."

"Is he the–" She broke off, not knowing if Liana wanted to talk about her injuries and who had caused them. "How did you get in here?" Amos had explained that someone had to have used the Void from a location to be able to return to that location through the Void. "I thought you'd only used the Void from the kitchen."

"That's where I went to, but your father was there so I had to stay in the Void since you don't want him to know about us."

When her phone rang, Claire declined the call without checking who it was. "You promised not to interfere."

"You expect me to let Wayne get away with

everything? The cuts might have healed, but I haven't forgotten them. Being able to heal quicker than a human doesn't mean less pain."

"He won't get away with anything, but we need to make sure he doesn't come after us, not just you." Her phone rang again and once more she declined the call.

"If he's dead he won't be able to come after anyone."

Claire's phone beeped, notifying her of messages. She had a feeling Roy wouldn't be happy with that solution. It didn't seem like a knightly kind of action. "Don't do anything until we all have a chance to decide what needs to be done." Her phone rang. She breathed out slowly. "Wait a minute." She glanced at the name on the screen before she answered. "Nate."

"What's going on? Why wouldn't you answer either of us or reply to our messages?"

"Everything is okay. Liana is here."

"Is she okay?"

Claire looked the girl up and down. "Nate wants to know if you're okay."

"I'd be better if you let me kill Wayne. I'll let the girl with him live. She wasn't part of it. Or at least I never saw her."

Before Claire could pass along the message, Nate

spoke. "Don't let her go after Wayne on her own. And what girl is she talking about? Was it Jennifer?"

In the background Roy spoke, clear enough for Claire to hear him. "Jennifer is as dangerous as her father."

Claire had no idea what to do. Everything seemed too complicated. Considering she'd wanted her dad to come home, she was now counting the days until he left. "Can we wait until next weekend to start sorting stuff out? Saturday, once my dad has gone." Her mum would be home on Monday so they'd better have everything dealt with before then. She was likely to want her to visit for a few days. Hearing footsteps, she started to ask Liana to disappear. The girl vanished before she could. "Come back when he's gone, Liana." She spoke the words even though she didn't know if Liana had remained nearby or left.

"When who's gone?" Nate asked.

Claire ignored Nate when her dad knocked on the bedroom door. "Come in, Dad."

"Did you want to ring me back in a minute?" Nate asked.

Darrell remained in the doorway. "I didn't realise you were on the phone."

Claire grinned. "It's only Nate."

"Tell him I said hello."

She repeated the words.

"I heard him. Tell him I said the same," Nate said.

"Do you two need to talk to each other?"

Darrell chuckled. "No need. I'm sure he'll be here one night before I return to work. Or several nights."

"Probably." She grinned, the problems momentarily fading at the familiarity of the moment.

"Tell him I'll be there tomorrow night. Mum will get over it," Nate said. "She should be used to me rarely being at home."

She relayed the message.

"When will I get to meet Roy?" Darrell asked.

She heard Roy's reply in the background and said, "Tomorrow night too."

"And his family?"

"I don't know." It was going to be difficult enough getting Roy inside without having to worry about keeping Wayne from knowing the entire family were entering her house.

Darrell nodded, turning away. He took a single step before facing her again. "Why is Nate's car here and yours isn't?"

"We swapped cars for a couple of days," she blurted out.

"Why would you do something like that?" Darrell asked.

She had no idea. The silence stretched out for what felt like minutes, but it had to have only been seconds before Nate gave her an excuse and she repeated it. "Nate doesn't believe my car is better than his. So I'm proving it."

Darrell slowly shook his head, a smile forming. "You pair have to turn everything into a competition." He walked away, this time not turning back.

Claire got off the bed, heading for the door to close it, running into Liana who came out of the Void. "Sorry."

Liana took a step away and closed the door. "Why did you want me to stay?"

"Come to dinner tomorrow night."

Liana looked startled, her expression rapidly turning suspicious. "Why?"

"Why not? Everyone else will be here."

"Tell Liana we'll talk about what to do with Wayne after dinner," Roy said in the background.

"Okay. What time?" Liana asked.

"Seven."

Liana nodded, then vanished.

Claire stared at the spot, wondering if the girl had left or if she remained in the Void. Trying not to breathe out heavily, she focused on the phone call. "When are you bringing my car back?"

"Dinner tomorrow night?"

"Why not swap at school?"

"We better not swap too soon after the excuse we gave."

"How did everything get so complicated? I didn't think it'd be this hard."

"Give it time. We'll figure it out and then things are sure to become fun."

They chatted a little longer until Nate said he had to go. Amos was back to train them. Claire placed her phone on the bedside cabinet, wishing she was with them. It wasn't fair they got to train while she was stuck at home.

Chapter Twenty-Four

The week passed quicker than Claire expected. Monday night dinner went better than she thought it would. Her dad told her he liked Roy, once him and Liana had supposedly gone to his place through the backyard. They had travelled through the Void from the laundry after they'd spent time in her room discussing what they should do about Wayne. Nate had stayed that night, spending the rest of the week between his home and the apartment with Roy.

Friday, Nate stayed the night and Saturday morning they stood in the doorway, waving as Darrell got into Rick and Tina's vehicle. The scent of dragon washed over Claire and she spun to face Liana and Roy, stepping inside with Nate so she could close the door.

"I thought he'd never leave," Liana said.

"All right. We've got today and tomorrow to get

this sorted. If everything goes right we'll only need today." Claire looked at each of them. "Is everyone ready to do their part?"

Nate grinned. "More than ready." He turned to Liana, holding out his hand. "I'll never get bored with how amazing it is to travel through the Void."

Liana took his hand, looking to Roy. "I'll be back for you in a minute." She vanished, taking Nate with her.

Claire stepped forward, wrapping her arms around Roy. "Are you sure your friend Amber will collect Wayne and Jennifer once we have them?"

"If she doesn't one of her dragons will. They won't be happy to learn he was plotting against her."

"I still think you should have rung and warned them."

Roy shook his head. "They would have taken over. And Ronan probably would have thought I owed him for his help. It's better this way. Amber isn't drawn into any trap Wayne might have set for her and we'll make sure it's safe before she comes to Brisbane."

Liana came out of the Void. "Hurry up. Nate is over there by himself."

Claire's lips momentarily met Roy's before she drew away, letting go of him so Liana could take him to the back of Harold's house. She was more than a little annoyed that it was left to her to distract Harold and make sure he stayed out of the way. Slipping her feet into her sneakers, that were at the front door, she stepped outside, closing the door softly behind her. She took in a deep breath, the smells of the area filling her senses. Nothing had changed. The neighbourhood was the same. Checking for traffic, even though she couldn't hear or smell any coming, she strode across the road to knock on Harold's door.

She knocked again, a little louder this time. Surely he wasn't asleep. He always rose early so he wouldn't miss a single thing that happened in the street. "Harold?" She heard footsteps inside. They were too brisk for them to be Harold's. Why was someone else coming to the door? Their plan hinged on it being Harold who answered. They didn't want him injured during the coming fight. As annoying as he was, he didn't deserve that.

The door swung open. "What?"

Claire stared at Jennifer, disliking the girl instantly. "Where is Harold?"

"He had a fall. I'm his granddaughter. I'm looking after the place until he's out of hospital."

She could smell him. A scent strong enough that Harold would be inside. Had they killed him? No, there was no smell of death. She forced a smile to her lips. "How thoughtful of you. Do you know how long he's expected to be in hospital?"

"No." Jennifer started to close the door.

Claire placed a hand on it, her smile widening as she thought of the perfect excuse. "He promised to lend me a book. I'm doing a project for school and I need to borrow it. Your great grandfather kept a diary and we need to use at least one primary source for the project."

"You'll have to come back when he's out of hospital."

"That's okay, I know exactly where it is." She pushed against the door, stepping forward when it opened further.

"I'm not about to let you take my great grandfather's diary until Har… ah… my grandfather tells me it's okay," Jennifer said indignantly.

"Jennifer? What's taking so long?"

Claire almost closed her eyes at the sound of Wayne's voice coming closer. Things were about to go horribly wrong and she had no idea what to do other than play along for as long as possible. "It's in his room." She slipped past Jennifer. "I'll only be a minute."

"Stop, or I'll shoot you."

Claire spun to face Jennifer, shocked to see the girl pointed a gun at her. Raising her hands, she stepped slowly backwards, further into the house. "You have a gun?" It was easy to sound incredulous.

"Jen-" Wayne broke off, drawing a gun of his own. "Where's Roy?"

A handful of words went through Claire's mind, most of them four lettered, but she was unable to speak a single one. There were two guns pointed at her and she had no idea what to do.

"I'm here." Roy rushed towards Wayne. He didn't reach him before Jennifer fired, blood staining Roy's light coloured shirt.

"No!" For a second Claire didn't realise it was her who called out. She was across the room and knocking the gun from Wayne's hand before she could think.

Chaos exploded around them. Several Knight Mages came out of the Void. More gunshots were fired. Nate and Liana were at the far end of the hallway while Claire stood at the beginning, Nate starting to run towards her.

"*Escape. Liana, take Nate and escape,*" Claire told them as arms restrained her, making it impossible for her to go anywhere. They were outnumbered and the Knight Mages had guns.

Liana grabbed hold of Nate who tried to push her away. They disappeared before he could escape her grip.

Claire mentally reached for Roy who was kneeling on the floor, a gun pressed to his head. *"I'm sorry. I didn't think about anyone being in the Void."*

"I'm to blame. I should have known better," Roy said directly to Claire.

Before she could say anything else to him, a cloth was pressed over her nose and darkness descended.

When Claire woke it was to find herself chained in a room that looked like a dungeon, right down to a barred window set high in a stone wall and a solid timber door with a barred window at head height. Light filtered in the window doing little to dispel the shadows.

Across from her was Roy, chained to another wall, the blood on his shirt dried. She struggled to her feet, mentally reaching for him. Fear raced through her. Why couldn't she speak in his mind? Next she tried to turn into a dragon, hoping the dragon strength would break the chains. Nothing happened. It was like the dragon no longer existed.

"Roy?" She couldn't keep the fear from her voice. She went as close to him as the chain would allow. It was too far for her to be able to reach him. "Roy."

Trying to slow her breathing she focused on her surroundings. The scents and sounds. She nearly collapsed in relief when she heard the beat of his heart. "Roy." His name came out a whisper. She was about to call to him again when she heard footsteps approaching.

Claire dropped to the floor, closing her eyes. She might be able to surprise someone if they came close. The footsteps stopped outside the door and she strained to hear anything else. All she heard was a steady heartbeat. Carefully breathing in deeply, she realised it was Wayne. If he came close she'd make his heart race in fear. Anger rushed through her. She should have let Liana have him. Too bad if Roy was offended or wanted him taken alive. At least he wouldn't now be chained in a dungeon with a gunshot wound.

Another set of footsteps came towards the door, stopping beside Wayne. She recognised the scent. It was one of the Knight Mages that had come out of the Void in Harold's house. There was a rustle then a click, the door swinging open with barely a sound. She wanted to open her eyes, but resisted. They weren't close enough and she didn't want to lose what little advantage surprise would give her.

"Here."

The Knight Mage spoke and Claire nearly opened her eyes to see what he was doing.

"You will owe me after this," the Knight Mage said. "My debt to you is paid now you have Roy. If you lose him again that's your problem. And if you want an audience with Fredrick once you've made the exchange that is also your problem. I want nothing more to do with this. I value Tobiah's life more than yours."

"Are you sure this other house hasn't been compromised?" Wayne asked.

"Nothing is certain in life." The Knight Mage paused a moment. "You and your daughter will help next time a client pays us to go after a dragon clan."

"I don't like the idea of working for dragons. We aren't mercenaries."

"They pay in gold. We can't afford to be picky when it comes to money. Not with all the upheavals amongst our faction. Besides, we're killing dragons. That's the main point. You can work in Tobiah's team."

"I'm not working for someone who's willing to give into kidnappers."

"Yet you are willing to use that tactic yourself."

"Exactly. I wouldn't be that weak." Wayne's voice was filled with disgust.

It took all of Claire's willpower to remain still. It wasn't weak to save those you loved. No matter what you had to do.

"What would you do if it was your daughter who was taken?" the Knight Mage asked.

"If it was by dragons I'd expect her to find a way to escape. She wasn't raised to be weak. She knows I'd never give into the demands of dragons. Even if they threatened to kill her."

Shock raced through Claire. He'd let his daughter die? How could he sound so certain he wouldn't give in and offer anything to have her back?

"Are you sure you won't use your dragon contacts so I don't need to go through Isaac to arrange the exchange?" Wayne came closer.

When he stopped, Claire heard the rattle of chains and peered through her eyelashes. She tensed, wanting to jump to her feet and tell him to leave Roy alone. But it wouldn't help. She couldn't reach Roy while she was chained to the wall.

"You have a nerve to ask me that again. You are the one who owes me." The Knight Mage's tone was frosty, tinged with disbelief. "You better not try and get out of what you owe me." He spun on his heel, striding out of sight.

Wayne unlocked Roy's chain from the wall and

slung Roy over his shoulder. Rising to his feet, he thrust his hand into the caged Pliethin hanging from his belt and vanished.

Chapter Twenty-Five

Her mouth gaping, Claire leapt to her feet. "No." The word was drawn out, more a moan than an actual word. She should have done something. She had no idea what, but anything other than pretend to be unconscious.

Wayne reappeared in front of her, without Roy. He drew a gun, pointing it at her. "Back away. I don't have to let you live. Only Roy is useful."

Her gaze firmly on the gun, Claire did as she was told. "Then why don't you let me go?"

"And have you cause problems for me?" Wayne unlocked the chain from the wall. "I wouldn't try and escape if I were you. Annoy me and I'll take it out on Roy."

She met his gaze, staring into ice blue eyes. There would be no mercy from him. She nodded, the movement feeling awkward.

"Hold out your hand."

She did as ordered, wanting to pull away from him when he took hold of her hand. Her gaze remained on the gun and she thought of Roy, keeping herself still when she wanted to attack.

Wayne took them through the Void, letting go of her hand when they came out in a cell, Roy lying on the floor. Wayne vanished again.

Claire hurried forward, dropping to the concrete floor to reach for Roy. He couldn't be… She pushed the thought away. His skin was warm, his heartbeat steady. Drawing in a shaky breath, she started to pull his shirt apart to check his wound.

His hand wrapped around her forearm above the manacle, stopping her. "Are you hurt?"

She shook her head, worried she'd burst into tears. "I thought you…" She couldn't say the word 'dead'. Her gaze was drawn to the blood on his shirt. The fear had lasted for a second or two. Long enough for her to listen for his heartbeat, but it had been the worst feeling. Some things even she couldn't voice.

"We have to get out of here."

"I can't." She shook her head. "I can't turn into a dragon. I don't feel like one anymore. What did they do to me?"

"It's the chains. They're the same as they used on

Liana. They deaden dragon powers. All dragon powers. Try and become a mouse."

"I can't. I don't know how." She momentarily closed her eyes. "We're right back where we started. Stuck in a cell." The scent of Wayne and Jennifer was behind her and she tried to rise and face them.

Roy pulled her to him, his grip on her tightening.

Jennifer held a gun. She pointed it at Roy. "It looks like I have the pleasure of keeping you a prisoner this time."

Wayne shifted the direction the gun pointed in. "We need him. If he tries anything, shoot the girl. Attach their chains to the rings set in the wall. I'll be back once I talk to Isaac and give him our demands." When Jennifer nodded, Wayne stepped into the Void.

Jennifer grinned. "Do something stupid. Go on. I'd love to shoot your girlfriend."

Claire tried to stand. Once again Roy prevented her. "I could be over there quicker than you can shoot."

"Want to place a bet on that?" Jennifer asked.

Roy pressed a hand against Claire's face, turning her to face him. "No. Don't do anything stupid." He leaned forward, pressing his lips to hers before whispering, "The bottle I stole from them is in my left pocket. Take it. I'll rush her and you use it on her."

"You can kiss her all you want," Jennifer said. "I don't care about you anymore. When you sided with dragons all I felt for you was disgust."

Claire drew back slightly, smiling at him. When his grip loosened, she pulled away, acting like she was about to take the bottle from his pocket. "No. You put her out." She spun, on her feet before he could stop her, rushing towards Jennifer.

The gun went off as Jennifer was slammed against the bars of the cell. "No!" Jennifer fought to escape, trying to aim the gun at Claire.

She kept Jennifer pinned against the bars, pain burning along her side, so great it took all her effort to focus on keeping Jennifer from escaping. "Roy." She heard a tearing sound behind her as she banged Jennifer's hand against the bars and knocked the gun from it.

Roy pressed a cloth to Jennifer's nose. "This wasn't the plan." He threw the cloth on the floor when Jennifer slumped forward, grabbing hold of Claire to drag her close. "I smell blood. Your blood."

She wanted to tell him not to hold her so tight. It hurt. But she didn't want him to let go.

"You have to change into a mouse. Before Wayne

comes back." Roy let go of Claire to check Jennifer over. "She has no key. Only the padlocks she would have used to attach our chains to the wall. You're our only chance of escape." He picked up the gun, tucking it into the back of his dragon leather trousers.

She backed away from him, shaking her head. "I can't do it. I've tried hundreds of times. I'm not a mouse."

"Nate can turn into a cat."

"He probably couldn't turn into a mouse."

Roy kept pace with her, stopping in front of her when she ran into the bars of the cell. "Do you want to die?"

His words arrowed through her, bringing to mind the fear she'd felt at thinking he was dead. "No." She could only whisper the word, caught up in the fear.

"Do you want me to die?"

She tried to pull away from him, not wanting to think about it a second longer. The world grew larger, Roy enormous, folds of cloth rising up around her and the chains falling to the concrete floor, seeming unnaturally loud. She scampered out of the way, trying to avoid being hit by them.

Roy scooped her up. "I knew you could do it."

She tried to reach his mind. It was impossible. She might not be chained, but he was. Squeaking, she looked over the edge of his hand, drawing back when she saw how far she was from the floor.

Roy placed his other hand over her, the chains rattling as he created a safe cocoon. "Escape. Call Uncle Amos and tell him where I am." He ran a thumb down her back before he placed her on the floor.

She looked up at him for a second, wanting to assure him she wasn't about to desert him. There was no way she could tell him so complex a message when he wore those chains. She rose on her back legs, gazing at him a moment longer before she dropped to all fours and scampered towards the door. She slipped under it, finding herself in a hallway. It was so much like the previous place that she began to think they were in the same house.

Forcing herself not to think of the possibility of ending up naked, she concentrated on becoming human. She should have checked to see if she'd left any clothes other than her hoodie behind. The change came easily, one she'd made many times from her dragon form. A shiver ran through her, the concrete floor cold on her feet, but at least she wore her dragon leather trousers and vest, blood continuing to trickle down her side. She checked the first room. It was empty, even the built-in wardrobe.

The same with the rest of them. Only the cleaning cupboard was filled and she glared at the bottles of bleach. She wasn't about to let them torture Roy.

Striding up the stairs, she checked the door. It opened. Breathing in deeply, she tried to figure out if any of the scents meant human. After a moment she decided none of them did. It didn't take her long to find that upstairs was empty. There was a handful of basic furniture, but there was no food in the cupboards and the fridge was turned off. It was a different place to the last one.

Spying a cordless phone, sitting in a cradle on a side table in the lounge room, Claire picked it up and checked the dial tone. She dropped into a nearby armchair, relief making her giddy. Then she realised it might not be relief. Blood coated her side. The wound in the flesh above her hipbone continued to bleed. She pressed her hand against it, hissing at the pain, blinking when her vision momentarily faded.

She started to dial Nate's number, the only one she knew off by heart, then realised she had no idea where to send him. Leaving the phone on the armchair, she ran to the front door, stumbling. The handle was difficult to open with the blood coating her hands and she staggered outside, looking for a street sign, or something that would tell her where she was.

The street was quiet, the corner two houses away. She took note of the number on the mailbox and ran to the corner, her breath coming in short, sharp bursts, the giddiness growing. Somehow she made it back to the lounge room, not sure if she closed the front door. She decided it didn't matter. Picking up the phone, she dialled Nate's number, stumbling towards the stairs leading to Roy.

"Claire! Where are you?"

Chapter Twenty-Six

Claire gave Nate the address, her words sounding like they'd been spoken by someone else. Reaching the door separating her from the cell Roy was in, she turned the handle. For a moment she thought it was locked, then remembered the blood on her hand. She wiped it on her trousers before trying again.

"Claire! Answer me."

"What?"

"I've been calling your name."

"You have?" She swung the door open, the distance between her and Roy seeming too great. Stumbling, she landed on the floor.

"Claire? What's wrong?" Nate's voice was filled with worry.

"It's okay."

"Don't give me that shit," Nate snapped. "Put Roy on the phone."

She stared across the room at Roy, seeing the fear in his eyes. "It's okay." The words were said for Roy this time.

Roy put his hand between the bars, holding it out to her.

She staggered to her feet, managing to cross the distance between them, letting Roy take the phone from her when she collapsed on the floor, leaning against the cold bars.

Roy gripped her hand. "Open your eyes, Claire. She was shot, Nate."

She struggled to open her eyes, but they wouldn't cooperate. Telling them everything was okay also seemed beyond her ability.

"I need to ring Amber. She can heal," Roy said. "Hold on, Claire." He squeezed her hand.

She held onto his hand, not wanting to let go. That was something she could do. Opening her eyes wasn't possible.

"Rian? I thought I rang Amber's number."

She tried to hear the other side of the conversation, but it was all she could do to hold onto Roy's hand and not let go.

"I need a healer. When will she be back? I also need her and Crystal to remove a set of chains, that deaden dragon power, from me. Wayne wanted to use me to capture Amber."

It took her a moment to realise Roy was asking her where they were. She repeated the address, the words seeming like a major effort. She finally managed to open her eyes and reached out to press her hand against Roy's chest. "It's okay." She stared at the bloody handprint she left on his shirt. "I'm sorry."

"Claire-" Roy broke off at the sound of footsteps pounding down the stairs.

She tried to turn and see who was coming. It was impossible. She remained pressed against the bars, gripping Roy's hand. When others moved her, she protested, Roy's hand drawn from hers. She tried to focus on the girl leaning over her, but the world seemed to have become blurry.

"I'm Crystal. Everything will be okay. We brought a healer and two mages who can break Roy's chains. We'll get him out of here. Amber would be angry if something happened to Roy because they were trying to capture her." Crystal pressed a hand against Claire's shoulder. "Stay still. It's easier if you don't move. The healer is only new at this."

She wanted to protest that she wasn't some lab rat to be experimented on, but the pain receded and she became aware of Roy leaning over her, taking her hand again, his chains gone. She smiled up at him.

"Wayne's in the Void, trying to reach Jennifer's side." Crystal rose to her feet, dragging Wayne from the Void, ripping the caged Pliethin from his belt.

Wayne aimed his gun at Claire.

She couldn't move. The world felt fuzzy and her body lacked energy.

Roy leapt forward, turning into a dragon. With a roar he landed on Wayne, slamming him into the concrete floor.

"Don't kill him," Crystal shouted, reaching out to Roy.

Rian pulled her away. "Let us take him. It was Amber he was after. He's ours."

It took Claire a couple of minutes to realise what was going on. She struggled to sit up, a young man helping her. "Roy." Her voice lacked the volume she wanted, but it was enough.

Roy turned to face Claire, becoming human as he moved towards her, his arms wrapping around her to drag her close, his shirt in tatters. "Claire." His tone was filled with relief.

This time, his arms didn't cause her pain and she tightened hers around him. "It's okay."

"Claire." Nate ran towards her. He stopped when

he saw she was in Roy's arms. Behind him was Amos, his gaze scanning the area.

She smiled up at Nate, holding out an arm, keeping the other one around Roy. "You're safe."

Nate gave her an awkward hug. "Liana is too." He drew back. "Who are all these people?"

Rian gestured two men forward. "Take Jennifer and Wayne to the dungeons. They can stay there until Amber and Ronan return."

Roy looked up, continuing to keep an arm around Claire. "Where are they?"

Rian shrugged. "Ronan had something he wanted her to help him with."

Crystal sent off the healer and the others that were with them, only her and Rian remaining. "I thought you didn't want to be a dragon. Wayne won't keep that news to himself."

"If you set him free, he's mine to kill." Liana came forward. "I owe him a great deal of pain."

Rian interrupted Crystal, who had started to speak. "Ronan won't allow him to live. No matter what Amber might want. He signed his death warrant coming against her like this."

Liana gave a single nod. "Good."

Liana's fierce comment brought to mind the conversation Claire had heard in the dungeon. She reached for Roy's mind. *"Do you trust these people? I heard something that might be important."*

"You can speak it. No matter what Amos says, they're my allies," Roy said.

Claire explained what she'd overheard in the dungeon. Her words brought silence.

"This can't be good," Crystal said.

"Thank you for sharing the information with us." Rian gave a single nod to Claire.

She returned the nod, feeling like she should say something, but not knowing what that would be.

Rian frowned. "The smell of rodents is coming from you. Your skin. Along with dragon. How is that possible?" His gaze went to Nate. "You smell of cat and dragon."

Amos stepped forward, pointing a finger at Nate. "You will say nothing." He turned to Rian. "They're ours. They belong to the Knights. Along with their secrets."

Rian inclined his head. "Ronan will want to know how you did this."

Amos crossed his arms over his chest. "Then he can ask if he wants to know. Doesn't mean he'll learn anything."

Rian stared at him for a moment before he inclined

his head again. He turned to Roy. "Everything is settled?"

"Yes." Roy rose to his feet, drawing Claire up with him.

She swayed at his side, wanting to collapse.

Crystal darted forward, hugged Roy and then did the same to Claire. She grinned, her gaze on Roy. "You'll have to bring your girlfriend to Temolae Keep. Amber will want to meet her too." She stepped back, taking Rian's hand, and disappeared.

Amos tried to tug Roy from Claire. "Time to go home."

Roy pushed Claire into Amos' arms. "Take Claire first."

"But-" She didn't have a chance to protest. Amos stepped out of the Void and into her laundry. She swayed when he let her go.

Swearing, he scooped her up and strode to her room, placing her on the bed.

She grabbed his hand when he tried to step away. "Not from in here. At least go into the hallway before you use the Void." She didn't want him to be able to come out of the Void into her bedroom. It was a pity she couldn't see into the Void like Crystal obviously could.

Amos slowly shook his head, but did as she said before vanishing into the Void.

Bubbles came running into her room, barking. He jumped on the bed and licked at the blood on her hand.

She tried to push him away. "Eww. That's my blood. Get away."

Nate entered her bedroom, grinning. "Looks like he's not going to wait until you're a mouse before having you for dinner." He grabbed Bubbles. "I'm going to tell Liana that we were created. She's asking a lot of questions and deserves some answers."

"Okay, but not the exact details." She struggled to sit up. "I need a shower."

"No. You need sleep." He set Bubbles down in the hallway, closing the door. "Go to sleep, Claire." He pulled the bed linens down then drew them up over her. "Shower once you've rested. You're likely to knock yourself out if you try and stand."

Opening her mouth to argue, a wave of exhaustion washed over her. She planned to only momentarily close her eyes, but fell asleep instantly.

Chapter Twenty-Seven

Claire woke feeling surprisingly rested. It was barely daylight, her room mostly shadows. When one of the shadows moved, she breathed in sharply, breathing out slowly when she realised it was Liana. "I'm glad you're here."

"I can't stay. I need to find out who paid to have my family killed. If Tobiah was the sword I want to know who wielded it."

Before Claire could tell Liana that didn't mean she had to leave them to learn the information, Nate burst into the room. She returned his grin. "Where's Roy?" She couldn't hear or smell him in the house. The three of them were the only ones, other than Bubbles, that were here.

"He's going to be annoyed he finally gave into his mum and went home. She's been ringing and texting him for hours. He barely spent a handful of minutes at home yesterday when Amos ditched him over there." Nate took out his phone as he spoke, sending a text. The phone beeped to notify him of a return message. He held up the phone. "He'll be here in less than a minute. His family will be with him. Both his uncles and Eliza."

Claire struggled out of bed. "I need a shower."

Liana glanced in the direction of the laundry. "Too late now."

She would at least meet them in the lounge room rather than in bed. Staggering out of bed, she ran her fingers through her hair. It was impossible. Knots and dried blood prevented her from improving the state her hair was in. She grabbed a dark, long sleeved shirt and drew it over her head, hiding most of the blood, and met Roy and his family in the hallway. "I was going to the lounge room."

Roy closed the distance between them, wrapping his arms around her, his lips meeting hers.

It took her a few seconds to be able to ignore Eliza's glare and return the kiss. She eventually drew back slightly to smile up at him. "I'm glad you're okay."

"Are we going to the lounge room or standing in the hallway all morning?" Amos demanded.

"I vote for the hallway." Nate grinned at Amos,

taking a step back when Amos took a menacing step towards him.

Claire tried not to smile. Even biting her lip didn't help. "Lounge room." At least there she could sit down. She felt a little shaky. She didn't know if it was from blood loss or meeting Eliza. The woman looked formidable. More fearsome than Amos. She didn't want to ever cross swords with her. Reaching the couch, she sank onto it, Liana on one side of her, Roy on the other.

Nate sat on the arm of the couch, next to Liana. "What now?"

Isaac sat in an armchair and looked at each of them. "Amos claimed you're our dragons."

"I don't know if you can call us dragons. They can't change into a third form like we can," Claire said.

"What about Amos' claim that you're a Knight?"

Claire took hold of Liana's hand. "All of us."

"*I don't need your charity,*" Liana said directly to Claire.

"*It's not charity. It might have been fanatical Knights who were paid to kill your family, but it was Knights. One of them might know information. Or know how to learn that information.*"

Liana met Isaac's gaze. "All of us." She gestured towards Roy. "But he's my ally. Not you. You don't have the scent of dragon as strong as Roy and Amos do. You aren't truly one. You're more Knight than dragon."

"You can trust Uncle Isaac." Roy grinned. "More than you can trust Uncle Amos."

"That doesn't say much since I don't trust Amos at all," Liana said.

Claire spoke before an argument could begin. Eliza didn't look impressed with Liana's comment about her brother. "What does it mean being one of your Knights?"

"We'll train you and you'll follow orders." Amos looked at Nate when he said 'orders'.

"I need to finish school," Claire said. "And how am I meant to live? I wouldn't think being a Knight pays all that well."

"That's where you're wrong." Eliza looked to Liana. "Dragon hoards can be profitable to find."

Nate stepped in front of Liana when she rose from the couch. "If we're meant to be on your side, we'll expect to be treated that way. We don't tolerate bullies."

Claire had risen from the couch at the same time as Nate, unable to stand in front of Liana because he'd been in the way. "What do you expect of Knights?"

Roy took her hand, turning her to face him. A

smile slowly formed. "What do you think they do? Haven't you listened to anything I've said?"

She returned his smile. "They protect."

Roy nodded. "We're the last line of defence between humans and a world they don't know exists."

Keeping hold of Roy's hand, Claire met Nate's gaze. She grinned at the same time as he did, facing Isaac before she spoke. "That we can do. We won't hunt dragons unless we know for certain they're in the wrong." She thought of Liana's family. "But we will protect those in need of it." She reached for Nate's hand. "Like we always have."

"Do I have your oath that you'll protect humanity?" Isaac rose to his feet, his gaze unwavering.

She held his gaze for a moment, thinking of the day she'd met Roy and the oath he'd given to protect her. She turned first to Roy, returning his smile, then looked at Nate who grinned, giving her the slightest of nods. Again she faced Isaac. "Yes." Her hands tightened on those she held, Liana at her back. Roy's words, from the day she'd met him, came to her. "I give you my oath that I'll protect humans with my life. My oath as a Knight and a dragon. And whatever else I might be." The words felt right, settling in and becoming a part of her like the beat of her heart, echoed by Nate and Roy, Liana whispering into her mind the word 'ally'.

"I'll expect you at the New South Wales headquarters each weekend and during school holidays." Isaac looked from Nate to Claire. "We'll figure out a cover story you can tell your families."

"Not Roy," Eliza said.

"He's not a child," Isaac said softly.

"If you get him killed." Eliza glared at her brother.

Isaac smiled, his gaze returning to Roy and those who stood with him. "You're not the only one who won't allow that to happen, Eliza."

"I'm not going to hide what I am anymore," Roy said. "You need to figure out what story you want to tell."

Eliza started to argue. Isaac interrupted her. "We've always volunteered to find out what to expect of anything new. They accepted that when Lydia became a Knight Mage so we could learn what they are capable of. They'll accept that when I tell them the three of you offered to learn about the new dragons."

Amos stepped forward. "Four of us." When Isaac nodded, Amos said, "This lot can keep an eye on Silas." He nodded to Claire and her companions.

"Lydia thinks it's Claudia," Isaac reminded him.

"Probably none of you are right," Eliza muttered.

"You aren't down there so you don't know what's going on." Amos stood toe to toe with his sister.

Claire let the argument fade into the background, turning to Roy. "Has anyone checked on Harold?"

"No, we forgot all about him," Nate said.

Claire looked down at herself. The blood wasn't that noticeable, her hair was probably a mess, but who knew what kind of danger Harold might be in. "That's what we should do first." She sent her thoughts to her companions. *"Before we get drawn into an argument that obviously can't be won."*

Roy chuckled softly as they headed towards the door. "You'll get used to it."

She had no doubt she would and was looking forward to every minute of it. But first, they had a human to rescue. She stepped outside, breathing in deeply, the scents of her neighbourhood familiar. Nothing out of place. Harold was alive. It was time to make sure he was also safe.

Free Ebook

Subscribe to Avril's newsletter and receive a free ebook. This ebook is exclusive to those on her mailing list. To find out more about this offer visit: www.avrilsabine.com/free-ebook

*

We value your privacy and will not sell, rent, exchange or loan your email address to third parties. Your information is confidential and you are under no obligation to remain on the mailing list and can unsubscribe at any time.

About The Author

Avril is an Australian author who lives with her family on acreage in South East Queensland. She writes mostly young adult speculative fiction, but has been known to dabble in other genres. You can find more information about her at www.avrilsabine.com where you can also subscribe to her newsletter to be kept informed about new releases, current projects, blog posts and exclusive news.

Titles By Avril Sabine

Book 2: Wyvern

Book 3: Surety

Book 4: Knight

Book 5: Mage

Dragon Mage- Young Adult Urban Fantasy (with elements of romance)

(Series two of Dragon Blood series)

Book 1: Promise

Dragon Blood Chronicles- Young Adult Urban Fantasy (with elements of romance)

(Companion series to Dragon Blood)

Book 1: Oath

Book 2: Betrayed

Guardians Of The Round Table- Young Adult Fantasy LitRPG

(Co-written with Storm and Rhys Petersen)

Book 1: Dexterity Fail

Book 2: Goblin Boots

Book 3: Singed Feathers

Book 4: Frog Mage

Book 5: Crystal Mine

Book 6: Cursed Harp

Rosie's Rangers- Young Adult Western Steampunk

(6 book series)

Book 1: Justice

Book 2: Vengeance

Book 3: Treachery

Book 4: Accused

Book 5: Wanted

Book 6: Corruption

Mark Of Kings- Children's Fantasy

(Upper middle grade/preteen)

(4 book series)

Book 1: The Arena

Book 2: The Island

Book 3: The Assassin

Book 4: The King

STAND ALONE SERIES

Demon Hunters- Young Adult Urban Fantasy/ Horror (with elements of romance)

Book 1: Blood Sacrifice

Book 2: Retribution

Book 3: Tainted

Book 4: Premonition

Book 5: Cursed

Book 6: Feud

Book 7: Extrication

Plea Of The Damned- Young Adult Urban Fantasy/Paranormal

(6 book series)

Book 1: Forgive Me Lucy

Book 2: Forgive Me Aiden

Book 3: Forgive Me Jena

Book 4: Forgive Me Kobe

Book 5: Forgive Me Marti

Book 6: Forgive Me Dawson

Realms Of The Fae- Young Adult Urban Fantasy (with elements of romance)

The Sword (short story in Like A Girl Anthology)

Heart Of Stone

Book 1: A Debt Owed

Book 2: Marked By The Hunt

Book 3: The Magic Collector

Book 4: An Unexpected Betrayal

Book 5: Imprisoned By Iron

Fairytales Retold (Short Stories)

Snow-White And Rose-Red

The Twelve Brothers

The Light Princess

Beauty And The Beast

Sleeping Beauty

Aschenputtel

The Golden Bird

The Frog Prince

The Death Of Koshchei The Deathless

Myths And Legends Retold (Short Stories)

Ion, Son Of Apollo

Sir Gawain And The Maid With The Narrow Sleeves

Princess Ilse, The Giant's Daughter

YOUNG ADULT NOVELS

Young Adult Fantasy (with elements of romance)

Elf Sight

Earth Bound

Young Adult Urban Fantasy

Stone Warrior (with elements of romance)

The Jungle Inside

Young Adult Contemporary (with elements of romance)

Through Your Eyes

The Ugly Stepsister

Perfect Little Princess

Young Adult Contemporary/Paranormal

Whispers In The Dark (with elements of romance and same sex relationships)

Over Too Soon (with elements of romance)

Young Adult Sci-Fi

Experiment X-One-Six (Urban Sci-Fi/Superheroes)

An Endless Dawn (Post Apocalyptic Sci-Fi)

CHILDREN'S BOOKS

Dragon Lord (Preteen/early teens) (Fantasy)

The Irish Wizard (Upper middle grade) (Urban Fantasy)

SHORT STORIES

Urban Fantasy

Eternally Late

Dealings With Joe

Glimpses (short story in That Moment When Anthology)

Fantasy LitRPG

(Set in the same world as Guardians Of The Round Table Series)

Tales Of Inadon 1: The Disc (Co-written with Storm and Rhys Petersen) (short story in Game On! Anthology)

Post Apocalyptic Sci-Fi

Compulsive Directive

NONFICTION

A Year Of Weekly Writing Exercises (Creative Writing)

Cooking For Families With Allergies (Cooking) (Co-written with Storm Petersen)

Tell Me A Story, Grandma (Memoir)

For the most up to date details on available titles visit:

www.avrilsabine.com/books/bibliography

Dragon Blood Series

To learn more about this series visit:

www.avrilsabine.com/series/db

BOOKS AVAILABLE IN THE DRAGON BLOOD CHRONICLES

(Companion stand alone series to Dragon Blood)

Book 1: Oath

Book 2: Betrayed

BOOKS SET IN THE SAME WORLD AS THE DRAGON BLOOD CHRONICLES

Dragon Blood- Young Adult Urban Fantasy (with elements of romance)

(5 book series)

Book 1: Pliethin

Book 2: Wyvern

Book 3: Surety

Book 4: Knight

Book 5: Mage

Dragon Mage- Young Adult Urban Fantasy (with elements of romance)

(Series two of Dragon Blood series)

Book 1: Promise

Disclaimer

This is a work of fiction. Names, characters, businesses, places, events and incidents are either the products of the author's imagination or used in a fictitious manner. Any resemblance to actual persons, living or dead, or actual events is purely coincidental. The opinions expressed or beliefs held are those of the characters and should not be assumed to be the opinions or beliefs of the author.